THE STORY OF
A COCKNEY
KID

by

RS LAWRENCE

Grosvenor House
Publishing Limited

This book is published by
Grosvenor House Publishing Ltd
Link House
140 The Broadway, Tolworth, Surrey, KT6 7HT.
www.grosvenorhousepublishing.co.uk

A CIP record for this book
is available from the British Library

ISBN 978-1-78623-556-5

CONTENTS

All names and characters in this book are fictitious and have no reference to any living person.

PROLOGUE

This story begins in 1928 when Miss Mary Ann Copeland married Mr Harold George Monk. Harold was called, by his friends and workmates, 'Harry'. He worked in a steelyard engaged in making iron girders for the construction industry. He had a good wage as a skilled man, earning four pounds seventeen shillings and sixpence per week. Mary was a seamstress employed by a clothes manufacturer in Millwall town, and as a top seamstress, was well paid. They had found a small, ground floor flat. It had a basic kitchen, consisting of a white ceramic sink with cold running water, also a gas cooker. Attached to the back of the flat was a washing room with a built-in cauldron for washing clothes. From there, a doorway led to the outside toilet. There was a small garden enclosed in a tall brick wall in a triangular shape. The lounge was small but cosy, with just one window which looked out onto the brick wall of the airy steps, leading to the lower front door. On the upper floor of the house were two bedrooms, one large double room, a smaller bedroom and a box room. On the landing there was also a toilet, shared with other tenants on the third and fourth landings. It was situated at the end of the landing, immediately above the garden toilet.

In the largest rooms there were fireplaces fitted with gas fires, with the gas meter alongside. The cost for a unit of gas was one shilling. All lights were gaslights, situated on all floors and corridors, but a supply of candles was kept in case they didn't have a shilling for the meter. The only disappointment was the area in which the flat was situated. It was in the run-down area of the docks, in the east end of London, on London's Isle of Dogs.

They settled down and were very happy for the next couple of years, then Mary told Harry that she was having a baby. Harry was delighted. They informed Mary's mother, who was also delighted. Her father told them that all medical expenses would be covered by him until after the birth, which was a great relief to both Mary and Harry, as it would be a big burden financially. The cost of living in England started to get expensive. Due to the Wall Street crash in 1929, there was money trouble throughout Europe. The crash of the American markets would have a terrible effect on other countries, particularly Germany, who had not yet recovered from the dreadful first world war. This led to a new political upheaval throughout Europe.

CHAPTER 1

WELCOME JAMIE

Mr and Mrs Monks' first child was born. The date and time was Wednesday, 12 noon, 15th September 1931. He was named James George. His mother loved him as only mothers can love their first-born. His father Harry loved him too, telling Mary how pleased he was to have a son. He had remarked, 'He looks like he needs ironing,' when he first saw his son, 'but he is beautiful.' His father was employed in an iron yard along the bank of the Thames. He was working on girders for the construction industry, earning the top wage of the day. Jamie had no idea what it was his dad was making them for as he was far too young.

Returning home with her new son, it was now a learning time for Mary. Mary settled down for the next eighteen months to a daily routine with baby Jamie until he was big enough to crawl, then learning to walk and looking for, and getting into, trouble.

Time passed and he had gradually grown big enough to go outside into the big world, and, like a typical boy, he found both friends and mischief. Jamie's mum now did homework and stayed at home most of the time. However, when she was going out, she always took him with her, both shopping or visiting her mother or friends, also when returning her finished work to the factory. She was intent on keeping him safe and sound in this dangerous part of London. The time would come when he could, and he would, go out on the streets alone, making and playing with new friends. Mary would do her best to keep him safe from the dangers of the street. She had no doubt that he would be just like the other children that played in the streets, making their own games. Mary loved this boy so much that sometimes it hurt.

Most nights, at bed time, she would sing a lullaby to him or ask Harry to tell him a story. That's how the first four years

1

passed. By the age of five, he was a street urchin, looking like the scruff, he was. New clothes were too expensive, so his mum either knitted them or altered other clothes. She got them from the second-hand shop on the corner of the street. The pawnbrokers' clothes were more expensive and there was no point in going there.

All his games were played in the street, mostly with a football or a tennis ball; the cheapest his mum could buy, or one he had found, or stolen. He made every effort not to lose it. Other games played were Hopscotch chalked on the pavement, or Tip Cat. This was a game made with wood. Find two pieces, one a stick two feet long and one about three inches long, sharpened at both ends. Place the short one on the edge of the curb and strike it with the other, and as it jumps into the air, try and hit it as far as you can. The one who made the longest strike could have a second or third go.

The road was the general playground, but sometimes he would wander into the council playground and on the swings or the seesaw. His mother warned him never to talk to strangers. If they tried to stop him, he was to walk away or run home, because there are bad people who steal kids. Sometimes he would have a game of Tag, which was played with several of the friends who came to Jamie's street, or he went to them. Every so often, when playing in the street, some form of traffic would come along; maybe the coalman with horse and cart, or the milkman doing his rounds, but if it was the rent-man, run and let Mum know he was about. Jamie had a wise street head on very young shoulders. He knew that Mary needed forewarning when the rent man was around. What he didn't know was why. There were very few motor vehicles in Jamie's day. The most traffic was an occasional bus. More often, it was a small car that tinkled like a bell as it drove along. That was the nurse, going to visit someone. He'd been told there were things called trams, but not here. Anyway, everyone got out of the road when a bus came along. He knew about trains, because he had a small clockwork train to play with at home.

CHAPTER 2

SCHOOL, AGED 5

Jamie had to start school at the age of five, because it was compulsory. Also, his mother was not going to let him grow up without a proper education, like so many children in the area. Although Jamie was very good at things like drawing pictures with chalk on the pavement, he could only print his alphabet and numbers, as taught by his mum. Five years passed with very little change except he grew and cost his mum several nervous attacks. He'd had most of the childhood illnesses and sicknesses, measles, mumps, tonsillitis, scraped knees and black eyes from fights in the street, usually with a friend, but they always made up afterwards.

Jamie remembered his first day at school, as it was the first day he had spent in the company of a lot of children he didn't know, and he was nervous. His mother, Mary, had always been with him during the day. She was always handy whenever Jamie needed her. Now she wasn't there. She had taken him right up to the school gate, then kissed his cheek, saying, 'Be a good boy, do as you're told, obey what the teacher tells you to do and tell me all about it at dinner time. I'll collect you this afternoon. I will be right here by the gate.' Then she gave Jamie a gentle push towards the school playground, which was now filling up with other children. Turning away, her self-control was hard to keep as she left him alone for the first time. Jamie, like all the other children, was looking around for the face of a friend. Seeing one, Jamie made his way and stood with him, until an adult came into the playground. The adult blew a whistle and with a loud voice told them all to go into the school hall and sit down. Once there, they were all instructed to go with another adult to different classrooms.

By midday, Jamie had settled down and made friends with several boys, most of whom lived locally. They would be able to meet after school. They had a great deal of toys to amuse them-selves with on their first day. The teacher sat among them and talked, always with a friendly face but showing that what she said was to be obeyed. Jamie was enjoying himself with the games and with his newfound friends.

Mary arrived, as promised, and as they walked home, Jamie didn't stop talking. He told her all that had happened and that he liked school. He had made some new friends whom he thought would be lifelong friends, as did they. (If only they could see the future.)

CHAPTER 3

GROWING UP

Two years passed and Jamie had progressed through the two school classes, no longer playing but learning. He still had his friends, but now the classes were for real learning. The teachers were now giving lessons on how to speak, read and spell in the English language. One teacher was teaching arithmetic. Jamie was beginning to understand that there is an awful lot to learn. The next subject Jamie was about to learn about was English history during the next school term. Now approaching his eighth birthday, his mum, dad and neighbours were talking about something called war, which seemed like it was going to come again, with the same people as in the big war some twelve years before he was born. He decided not to worry about that, as his mum was preparing to go on their annual trip to the hop fields in Kent during the summer school holiday. This was usual for most of the families in the area. They would be in the countryside for three or four weeks, in late August and early September, when it would be sunny and warm. Although he knew he would be able to have some fun, Jamie also knew he would be helping in the hop field alongside his mum and several other women, who were his mother's friends.

On the day of leaving for the hop picking, they loaded up the lorries which came to take them to the hop fields in Kent. There was enough room for several families and all their equipment in the large furniture removal vans. On arrival, the farmer took them to a long row of black, corrugated iron huts, one of which Mary went into. For the rest of the day, it was settling in, making the beds by filling palliasses with straw, making mattresses, then getting a fire going for a meal. First the iron trestle had to be erected, then the fire ring of stones, then, and only then, could

5

the fire be laid and made. It took some time before a meal was ready.

They would have to start work on the Monday, but had Sunday to get things right, and to get ready for work. Some of the families walked into the village for church, but Mary didn't and Jamie stayed with her, just relaxing in the sunshine. On the Monday, Jamie watched as the farmhands came with a tractor, pulling a flatbed wagon onto which the ladies put their children, then got on themselves. The wagon was then taken to the fields where the hops were trailing from a kind of netting. There were several large canvas troughs, around which the ladies stood, ready for the bines to be brought down from the overhead wires. The farmhands with long poles came and pulled the unpicked bines down from the high wire frame for the pickers; some of the bines fell onto the women and they looked adorned, with them hanging around their shoulders. They then began the job of stripping the hops from the bine into the large canvas trough. After a while, the farmhands would come with a basket and scoop the hops out, counting the scoops as they tipped them into a large, high sided barrow before taking it away. Jamie never found out where the hops went. It was four weeks later that the hop picking was finished. The fields then looked bare, with only poles and wires stretching from them, forming what looked like a large net, just hanging there.

On the first weekend after the hop picking was finished, Jamie, with his mum, several of her friends and their children, were going to the village of Hook Green, in Kent. As they walked down the lane, a cyclist pulled up beside them. Everyone stopped. The cyclist then told the ladies, 'England has declared war on Germany,' (that was on the 3rd September 1939). There was no panic, just a little excited talk about what might happen. Then they just carried on to the public house for their usual Sunday drink before returning for dinner. Jamie sat outside with a lemonade and a large arrowroot biscuit with several other lads and just wondered, what is war? He had heard about the wars in history class at school but had no idea what was going to happen. Some of the other boys were saying that it meant fighting with a country called Germany, and that they would all join the army when they were big enough.

That night, there was a gathering of the ladies. Jamie was told to go to bed, but curiosity got the better of him and he hid close by. The women were talking about war and how terrible it was last time. Jamie didn't stay long but went to bed and slept soundly.

Later, when they had returned home, Jamie asked his dad, Harry, about joining the army and was told that he would have to grow up before that could happen. Jamie decided to think about it again when he was big enough. For now, there was that apple tree in the garden of the empty house that Jamie had been watching as he came home from school. He had pointed it out to his mother, as it was on the other side of the street. The house was in a terrible state, but the garden had fruit trees growing. The apples would go to waste if he couldn't get them, and food could not go that way. Jamie's mum and dad could always eat them. They were on the other side of the road and some were ready and red, which looked most inviting. Jamie and a friend decided it was time. That evening, in the dusk before their mothers started calling them in, they cleared the hedge and were in the garden and up the tree, putting apples in their pockets. They were joined by other lads who came over to see if they could scrump some of them. Jamie was up in the tree collecting the ripest looking apples when Mary appeared, standing looking up at him. Jamie wondered, how did Mum get there? she said nothing, just pointed to the top of the tree, then said, 'Jamie, that one.'

When he finally came down with the apples she wanted, it was getting dark and they made their way home. Jamie never did learn how Mary got into the garden (he had forgotten that the front entrance had no hedge). The next day, the school holidays were over and on Monday Jamie would go back to school.

CHAPTER 4

EVACUATION

The school had been told to talk to the parents about the safety of the children in the coming months, and that the government wanted to reintroduce evacuation. It was now that Jamie thought things were changing. There was talk of sending children away to safe areas, and Jamie was to be one of them. What was evacuation and why was he going to be sent away? Jamie wanted to know. The teachers at school tried to explain that because of the danger of war, the children were being sent on holiday away from any trouble that could come.

When Jamie went home, Mary had the job of telling him what the trouble might be, that she wanted him to be kept safe and that this was the way to do it. Not many days later, Mary was packing a battered old suitcase, at the same time telling Jamie that it wouldn't be long before he was home.

Two days later, it was time for the children to leave. Long streams of them were walking to the school, full of wonder and not a little fear. Jamie was in his Sunday best: his jacket which had elbow patches sewn on, as well as his patched short trousers. The patches were well done. He had his cardboard gas mask box hanging around his neck and a small brown paper bag, with a jam sandwich for the journey. The old, battered suitcase, which was heavy, he struggled with, but he wouldn't give in. He felt embarrassed as his mother tried to kiss and hug him. He felt he was a big boy now. A teacher came and tied a label on his jacket collar and told him to get on the bus, as they were going off to the railway station. Jamie did kiss his mother then; just did as he was told, his mind in a whirl with all the activity and confusion. He wanted to know: where am I going and for how long? No one had told him what was going to happen when he got to wherever they were going. This would be something completely new. He was going on a train, but what were trains really like? He had only heard of them, but never seen a real one, only a toy. Jamie saw his first train on arrival at the station. It was big and noisy, and to his small size looked decidedly gigantic, and he was going to get on it. The train looked alive with billows of steam shooting out of it. It had a kind of sound as it stood there waiting to go, kind of like a clock.

After a lot of jumping about and hissing, it got underway and started on its journey. Jamie had managed to sit by the window, listening to the sound of the train wheels on the rails making a clickity-clack. Jamie was watching the countryside roll by. He found the green fields wonderful, and there was so much of it, much more than in the park by the foot tunnel, alongside the Thames.

CHAPTER 5

THE FARM

Jamie had calmed down and any fear he had he had hidden when he had got on board and sat down, along with several other boys and girls. Some were crying, others just sat and looked lost, others were talking nervously. Jamie did just as the teacher had told him; he sat and looked out of the window.

Some time later, as he was watching the countryside rolling past the windows, the train slowed and then came to a station and a juddering stop. The teachers hurriedly made the children collect their cases, or did it themselves for the little ones, and made everyone in Jamie's class get off the train. They were told to line up as if they were in the playground, in twos, then the train blew its whistle and started off, leaving them behind. The teacher got them started marching towards the village houses down the road.

Eventually they came to a building where they were shown into a hall and told to sit on the floor. Then a lady gave Jamie and the other children a drink and a cheese sandwich. Some were given water or an orange drink, others were given milk and something to eat. As the children sat on the floor, the teachers were looking around the village, trying to find them somewhere to live, with the ladies and gentlemen of the village, with whom a child, or two, would stay, possibly until the war was over. Several people came into the hall and wandered around, looking at the children sitting there. Jamie was sitting with a boy he knew very well. He waited until a man and woman came and asked Jamie if he would like to come with them. Jamie got up and they went to the teacher, who made a note and told Jamie to go with a Mr and Mrs Wilson to their farm.

Jamie picked up his case and followed them out. The man led him to a horse and cart standing close by. Mr Wilson, a big, strong man, picked Jamie up and put him on the seat, then put his case on the back of the cart. The cart had a strange smell, something like the corn chandler at home, where his mum used to take him. Jamie sat next to Mrs Wilson, the man's wife, who had already climbed onto the cart. Mrs Wilson was a bit on the chubby side, but warm and friendly. She told Jamie that her son had been called up into the army and he was away from home just now. They started to drive down the lane and Jamie thought the sight of the horse's backside rocking from side to side quite different to anything he had seen so far.

It took quite a while to reach the farmhouse where he was going to stay as an evacuee. Jamie sat still, looking at the farmhouse. It was a long, low building with white painted windows and a door with a porch, with some type of climbing plant all over it.

They had stopped in a big yard, with a large barn on one side, a cage with chickens all wandering about on the other. Mrs Wilson gave Jamie a kindly hand on his shoulder to bring him back to reality. Jamie did as he was bid and climbed down from the wagon, collecting his case and followed Mrs Wilson into the farmhouse. As he entered, a black and white dog came bounding up towards them, passed Jamie and went to Mrs Wilson, then turned and came back to Jamie, who stood still, just the same as at home. If a strange dog came up to you, you stood still, just in case. Mrs Wilson settled the dog, then took Jamie to a room upstairs and in a kindly voice told him, 'This is your room, Jamie.' He now had a bedroom. It would be his own while he was living there. To Jamie, this was all so new. Jamie just stood and looked at everything in the room. A proper bed with snow white sheets folded back and a colourful cover. This was his. Mrs Wilson told Jamie he was not sharing with anyone. 'Wow,' was all he could say as he sat in an armchair.

Later, Mrs Wilson told him he would be starting at the village school in two weeks because a new lady teacher had finally been engaged. The school room was in the village hall but in the meantime, he could wander about and get used to the farm. At first, Jamie was intimidated by the animals, especially the Shire horse that towered high above him.

Jamie started school just two weeks later. Now the hall was lined with rows of little wooden benches with a slate and chalk on each seat, all facing a blackboard. The teacher's desk was in front. An elderly lady sat there, who was the new teacher, brought out of retirement. It had been a long walk from the farm down a country lane. Jamie wasn't used to being in such a strange world. He was a town boy and the country seemed odd, empty and eerie, especially walking in woody areas.

After three weeks spent in the country, it was near the end of September, and the beginning of Autumn. Mr Wilson was very busy and needed help on the farm, and Jamie soon found that he would be expected to help, as there were still some harvests to be brought in. This had to happen before the bad weather of winter started. Particularly important was the potato crop. Jamie was put to work with the other farmhands and soon found out what hard, backbreaking work this was. School was suspended for the afternoons and most of the bigger children were out in the fields helping with the potato picking, with the teacher in charge. Bent almost double and scratching about in the dirt to find the potatoes that the machine had turned out, everyone was working, picking them up and putting them in baskets. For some of them it was just fun, but for Jamie, it was new and hard work. Jamie found that after an afternoon in the field, his back and legs, along with his shoulders, hurt. He was stiff and had a lot of aches and pains.

They finished work and he staggered back to the farm. Jamie was hobbling as he walked. Mrs Wilson saw that Jamie was hurting and got the tin bath out. Water was put on to be heated, and it was soon ready. Mrs Wilson made Jamie get undressed and into the hot bath. There she made him soak for a while. Now Jamie had only ever been bathed by his mum, and here was a strange woman, doing what Mum always did, but he was hurting so much and was so tired, he just didn't care.

Mrs Wilson gave Jamie his dinner as soon as he was finished. He put on his nightshirt, climbed upstairs and fell into bed. It was the cockerel that woke him up as the dawn was breaking. As he turned over, he wished he had never seen a potato and didn't want to see another for a long time. He had a short lie-in until

Mrs Wilson called him to get up, as his breakfast was ready for him. Jamie thought, porridge or bread and marge, as he made his way downstairs to the kitchen. There he found Mr Wilson and Mrs Wilson; she was by the oven cooking and the smell of bacon made his mouth water. She put plates in front of Mr Wilson and Jamie and there was an egg, bacon, fried bread and tomatoes. Jamie just looked and sat still, then looked at Mr Wilson. Mr Wilson stopped, with his fork halfway to his mouth, and said, 'Jamie, that's your breakfast. You can eat it, but if you want something else, you'll have to say.' Jamie didn't need to be told twice, he just started to eat. He had never tasted bacon before, this was a real treat, and very new for Jamie. A cooked breakfast was something that only Dad ever had. Mr Wilson was saying that he was going to bring in the cattle for milking. Jamie could come along and help if he wanted, before going to school. This was another new experience for him, following Mr Wilson, trying to forget his sore legs and back from yesterday.

Mr Wilson led him onto the fields. It felt strange; the grass was soft to walk on, not like a pavement or road. Mr Wilson started calling out very loudly, 'Home, Home.' Jamie asked why. Mr Wilson told him that the cattle knew what it meant, as they were all heading straight for the sheds. They knew the way. Mr Wilson explained that the call meant for them to go to the milking parlour. Jamie asked, as he followed, "How do they know the way?" Mr Wilson told Jamie that they knew there was fresh hay and cattle pellets for them in the milking parlour.

Jamie went into the milking parlour. Inside the parlour it was bright and clean and divided into stalls by metal frames. Only some cows went into the parlour, the others waited outside. The cows inside went straight into one of the stalls and started to eat the hay and pellets in the feeding troughs. Mr Wilson put a contraption onto each cow at this end of the row and the other farmhand, named Tom, did the same at the other end. They met in the middle as the contraption started to milk the cows automatically. Jamie was impressed and full of wonder at all this. He stood and watched them, then said, 'Mr Wilson, I have only seen milk in a bottle and I thought that's where it came from.' Mr Wilson said,

'Now you know better, Jamie me lad. Jamie, not only does milk come from cows but almost everything we eat is nurtured or grown. Corn is grown and later turned into flour for bread. Many other grasses are cereal. These are harvested and turned into food. Also things like potatoes, cabbages, Brussels sprouts, peas and many other vegetables must be grown. That's what farming is about, Jamie.'

When they had been walking towards the animals earlier, Jamie had felt anxious. The cows were big and they had all turned and looked at him and those horns looked dangerous, which had left him feeling a little frightened. The cows were only a little smaller than the big Shire horse in the field behind the farmhouse. Jamie had felt tiny when he had stood by that giant horse, as he only reached as high as the horse's knees. It had towered above him. Jamie felt today had been better than school, and that he had learnt a lot and hoped there was more he could learn. Now, after the experience of the morning, he felt a great deal safer with the animals.

CHAPTER 6

NEW ARRIVALS

It was a Friday afternoon when three young ladies arrived. Now Jamie knew why a lot of work in the big barn had been done. They were going to be living in the barn loft, which had been made into a kind of flat. They were going to live and work on the farm for Mr Wilson. Jamie saw them all later when he came home from school, then found out that the women were in the Land Army. They weren't soldiers, even though they had uniforms. He thought they looked very smart with their brown trousers and green jumpers and they wore hats that made them look extra smart. He noticed that when one of them spoke, she sounded just like him. She had the same sound in her voice. When she was speaking, he felt like he was home. She must have come from London, the same as himself. It wasn't long before he got to know them. They were now Mr Wilson's wartime workers.

A letter from his mum arrived on the Saturday. Mrs Wilson read it to him. The letter told Jamie that sometime soon he would have a brother or sister. She would tell him about this later. She also told him about the air raid shelters that were being built, also about the sound of the warning siren that was called by most people, 'Moaning Minnie', and that Dad was now in the AFS (Auxiliary Fire Service). So far it was still quiet in London, no air raids. She was hoping to come and see him later, if Dad could afford the fares. She wanted to know, how was he doing at school? Was he keeping up with lessons? She would write again soon, she promised. Jamie thought it wasn't a long letter, but at least it was a letter.

CHAPTER 7

THE LEARNING CURVE

Every time a letter arrived, he had to ask Mrs Wilson to read it to him as he couldn't read joined-up writing. He could read printed words better. When he wanted to write to his mum and dad, he always printed, but he found it hard to explain what he had been doing, because he didn't know the words for the different plants that were grown on farms. That's why he had to ask Mrs Wilson for her help, as he didn't have enough words to explain. His letter told his mum how he was out with Mrs Wilson, going around the lanes picking wild fruit; things he didn't know the names of. Mrs Wilson named them all for him, they were sloes, damsons, blackberries, also some wild Victoria plums. Jamie told his mum about the way Mrs Wilson saved them and called them preserves. Then there was the apples time and the sour apples called crab apples. He told her he never seemed to stop learning about the countryside, except when at school. He had learnt his times tables, right up to twelve. The writing lessons on a slate with chalk weren't going as well (also the scratching of the chalk on the slate set his teeth on edge) and he wondered when they would teach him joined-up writing, so he could write home, 'just like you do, Mum.' Sometimes, at night, he dreamt he was going home. He ended by telling her how much he loved and missed her, and wanted to tell to her face how much he loved her and missed her when she cuddled him.

The harvests had been brought in and school had reopened in the afternoons. Now Jamie was working hard with his lessons. The Land Army girls were doing farm work, along with the young village boy Tom, who had recently left school, as he was 14 and could no longer go to school. This was his first job as a farm hand, and how he loved farm work, like his father before him.

Mr Wilson decided that Jamie should learn that farming continued regardless of the weather or time of year, and that the autumn was a very busy time, with things like ploughing. Mr Wilson told him that the ploughed fields would be left for the rains, then the frosts would break up the frozen clods of earth, ready for the next job on the field, called harrowing. All this was getting the land ready for the spring sowing. Also, during late autumn, the hedges had to be trimmed and repaired. All these things had to be done by Christmas, which was only two and a half months away. Jamie wasn't expected to do these things, it was just part of his country education, but he could help if he wanted to. Mr Wilson would show him and teach him.

Jamie was now nine years old, as it had been his birthday on the 15th of September. Jamie had been disappointed that his mum had been unable to come and see him. Jamie now wondered if she would be able to come at Christmas. If so, would she be able to stay at the farm? Mr Wilson told Jamie she would be welcome and that she could stay over the holiday if she wanted to. Jamie fervently hoped and prayed his mum would be able to visit as he was longing to see her. It had been some six weeks since he had left home.

CHAPTER 8

NEWS FROM HOME

A letter arrived. Jamie sat down to try and read it but had to ask Mrs Wilson for help. It read, 'Dear son, you now have a baby brother and it will be a while before I can travel, but I will try as soon as I can to visit. Everyone went to the air raid shelters recently as the siren sounded, but nothing happened and no shooting so far. Dad said, "It's a war of nerves." We are ever so pleased you like it on the farm, and we look forward to visiting you later. Hope you had a very happy birthday. We didn't forget, we thought about you lots. We will try to see you as soon as possible. Lots of love, Mum and Dad.'

Jamie was happy they were still thinking about him but wished that they could have come and seen him on his birthday. The letter was meant to cheer him up, but he felt depressed, as he was just a little homesick, needing a hug from his mum. As much as it was good living here, it was not quite the same as home. He missed all the games he played in the street and the friends that he played with. Being able to go to the river and the slipways, climb on the barges, even being chased by the policeman if he saw them playing on the barges. Jamie even missed the clump his mum would give him when he was up to mischief and got caught.

CHAPTER 9

LEARNING ABOUT MONEY

Mr and Mrs Wilson told Jamie they would take him shopping later that week. They would take him to the market in Chipping Norton. Mrs Wilson told Jamie she needed to buy him new clothes as he only had the clothes he had brought with him and they were getting too small, as he was growing. They needed replacing before winter set in. For Jamie, it was his first time choosing new clothes. It was to be a treat for him and he was looking forward to choosing with Mrs Wilson. They would be new, not from the second-hand shop on the corner of the street at home. Although, some of those clothes had been nice. His mother had always wanted for him to have new clothes, 'but money is always too tight,' she had told him, and he had never been bothered by this, but this was different.

Mr Wilson had given him a ten-shilling note because Jamie had helped him on the farm, and he felt Jamie deserved some pocket money. This was something Jamie had never had before. He had never had any experience with money, he had only ever had a florin or pennies from his mum, when she had sent him to the corner shop for something she wanted. He thought he might be able to get something for his mum, if it was enough money.

It was on the third Wednesday of the month. Jamie was told that it was market day and they would be going early, and for him to get ready. Mr and Mrs Wilson harnessed up the horse and wagon. Mr Wilson left instructions with the Land Army girls, then picked Jamie up and put him on the driver's seat where Mrs Wilson was sitting. Mr Wilson then joined them. All three sat together and away they went.

This really was a very special day for a London kid, as they headed through the village of Haythrop, then joined the Banbury

19

road heading for Chipping Norton. Jamie was looking at everything as this was his first major trip away from the farm since he had arrived, only a couple of months ago. It seemed like he'd been there forever. They got to the crossroad and crossed to the top of the hill that runs down to the town. Jamie was looking all around, enjoying the sound of the iron clip-clop of the horse's hooves on the road surface.

As they entered Chipping Norton town, Jamie noticed that there seemed to be two road levels, an upper road which had a row of shops, and a road lower down where the market was, all colourful shades with a lot of people walking around. Mr Wilson stopped and Mrs Wilson got off and helped Jamie down. She said, 'We're going to the shops. We will meet you in the market at our usual place, The Chequers. OK?' Mrs Wilson then took Jamie's hand and they walked towards the shops. Jamie saw Mr Wilson nod his head as he started off.

They went into a large store with a lot of different things on show and a delightful homely smell of stuff Jamie didn't know. The clothes were hanging up around the walls and on rails. The first thing Mrs Wilson bought for Jamie was a night shirt, then under clothes, vests and pants, then two pairs of trousers, four pairs of socks, a woolly hat with a bobble on the top, reddish brown in colour, then two checked shirts of heavy cotton, a heavy jacket and a topcoat that was waterproof. She also bought him a pair of wellington boots. All this was in preparation for the coming weather in winter and spring, she said. A complete outfit! Jamie felt like jumping for joy at all this new clothing. He thought, Mum could never afford such things. Jamie suddenly began to wonder about the money. He asked Mrs Wilson if she wanted the ten-shilling note Mr Wilson had given him, to pay for the clothes. Mrs Wilson explained to Jamie that the government gave her an allowance towards his keep and she had bought the clothes he needed out of that, and no, the ten-shilling was his; Mr Wilson had said 'You should have some pocket money, for helping on the farm.'

Mrs Wilson took Jamie into a tearoom and ordered tea and cakes. Another treat for Jamie: cakes and cream. Wow! As they sat there, Jamie suddenly asked Mrs Wilson if he could buy a book. They finished their tea and Mrs Wilson took him to a shop that sold all sorts of stationery. Jamie stood and looked around in sheer wonder at the amount of books available. After several minutes, he saw what he wanted. He picked up a school exercise book, then some pencils. He was about to ask the woman behind the counter if he could have them, when he saw a book with a picture of an 'A', indicating that it was an alphabet book. This was what he had in mind. It showed the large printed 'A' and the small script letter 'a'. He wanted it, so much. He asked how much it cost and the lady told him that all three items cost eleven and a half-penny. Looking at Mrs Wilson, Jamie gave the lady the ten-shilling note. He was about to walk away when the lady called him back as she put the items in a bag, telling him to hold out his hand. She gave him his change of nine shillings and a halfpenny.

Jamie just stood and looked at all the money in his hand. He turned and asked Mrs Wilson if it was right. She looked and checked the money in his hand, told him it was. Jamie stood for a moment, then asked, 'Can I buy some sweets?' Mrs Wilson took him to another shop which sold sweets, but there was a big choice. Jamie bought some boiled sweets. Looking around, he saw that the shop was also a post office. He asked the lady behind the counter wire cage if he could buy a stamp. Upon her reply, 'Yes,' he bought a one-penny stamp. All told, he spent four and a half pence and still had eight shillings eight and a half pence left.

A little later, Mrs Wilson was looking at the stalls when she picked up a box, paid the man in the stall something then put the object in her bag. It had cost her tuppence. Jamie wanted to buy something for his mum and asked if Mrs Wilson would help him. Mrs Wilson then took him to a chemist shop, where she suggested perhaps a bottle of fragrance, costing one shilling and sixpence, would be something his mother would like. Jamie thought this was a good idea. He'd get that for his mum. Now he also had a sister. 'What for her?' he asked. Mrs Wilson was a mother and knew what was coming with a new child. She told Jamie that a teething ring would be a very useful thing for the baby, with bibs. Jamie decided to follow her suggestion. They found them and

Jamie picked one of each up, then went to the counter with Mrs Wilson to pay for them. The scent cost one shilling and eleven pence and the teething ring and bib cost ninepence. He had spent two shillings and eightpence.

He was happy and couldn't think of anything else, plus he was getting tired. They made their way to where they would meet Mr Wilson, at The Chequers pub.

It wasn't long before the clip-clop of the horse and the rumble of the cart came and stopped. They both climbed aboard. This time Jamie got in the back and lay down on a bundle of hay, looking at the blue sky. He became aware that the cart had stopped and opened his eyes. He was home again, at the farm. He thought to himself, what a wonderful day! That Wednesday wasn't finished for Jamie, as shortly after dinner, Mrs Wilson asked about the money he still had in his pocket. She sat with him and they counted it out. He had two shillings and sixpence left. Mrs Wilson produced a box that had a slot in the top and explained that it was a money box where he could put his money until he needed it. She told Jamie it was his. It was his belated birthday present. Jamie thanked her and gave her a hug, just like he used to do with his mum.

CHAPTER 10

A TIME OF CHANGE

The month had moved into October and the weather was changing. It was turning dull grey and threatening rain. The month was not looking good. Jamie learnt that whatever the weather it was still a very busy time, making sure the chickens were safely housed with a good dry nesting area within the barns. As eggs were rationed, there had to be a good collection sent to the Ag. & Fish dept. The barns had to be made safe from foxes. Sometimes even a stoat or polecat took a chance, but they preferred the rats and mice. These were in competition with the barn owls who hunted the mice and had taken up residence in the barn. Moving the cows under shelter, also the same with the horses. All the barns had to be made ready for the winter storage.

Jamie now did very little work on the farm. Mr Wilson had shown him a rabbit round, in which he was shown how to set traps and snares to catch rabbits, which were a pest for farmers, but very good for eating. These had to be cleared early before breakfast and school. Jamie, most mornings, came home soaked and had to change before going to school and getting wet again.

The weeks rolled on towards November. Jamie was remembering what Mr Wilson had told him, how his mum could stay at the farm, if and when she visited. Jamie wondered, would she come? Every day he looked for a letter from home as Christmas was only a few weeks away.

His very first Christmas away from home and family. It seemed an age ago when he had first arrived at the farm, but it had only been three months. He was on tenterhooks, wondering.

November arrived and school remained much the same, only now it lasted all day. The teachers were trying to get a school play going for Christmas. Jamie was to be a reindeer along with six other boys, pulling a sleigh with Father Christmas in it. His teacher, Mr Stevens, was to be Father Christmas. (Mr Stevens was elderly and rather rotund and would look very much like Santa Claus in the fancy dress.) Jamie was looking forward to the play and wishing his mum could be there.

Lately he had become interested in other subjects at school, geography and history, but books were rather scarce. Mr Stevens was the teacher for both these subjects, and because of Jamie's questions, had started giving Jamie individual lessons. Jamie had started trying to write in longhand, which he had practically taught himself, practising using the book he had purchased; copying each letter, keeping the pencil on the paper and joining the letters. Jamie had a lot of help from Mrs Wilson. His efforts were not very neat, but his letters were joined up and he was very proud of himself. He was going to try and write a letter to Mum and Dad in his best hand. Mrs Wilson sat with Jamie as he wrote his letter, telling his mum he was in the Christmas play. He hoped she could come and watch. He also told her all about the work going on at the farm. Also, that he had his job getting rabbits in from his snares and traps each morning and that he collected mushrooms. Mrs Wilson had taught him which were good to eat and which were poisonous. Mushrooms came up early each morning when the mist was on the grass and it was damp, but not so at this time of the year. He told her that Mr Wilson had given him ten shillings as his month's pocket money and wage, and he was saving it up. But if she needed it, he would send it to her. Maybe she could use it for her fare, to visit. He told her he loved her and his brother, and wanted to see his dad as well. He'd love to see them all. He had a long way to go with his spelling.

Later in the evening, Mrs Wilson was very busy in the kitchen making pies, cakes and many other things Jamie had never seen before. All sorts of preserves were brought out ready for use at Christmas, which was now only a few days away. As usual, Jamie watched for the postman and this morning there was a letter for Mrs Wilson. After she had read it, she called Jamie over and told him to sit down. Mrs Wilson told Jamie that the letter was from his mother, and that due to problems in London, she was coming to stay for little while. Mr Wilson was going to the Chipping

Norton railway station in the morning and Jamie was to go with him. Mr Wilson did not know what Mary looked like and he needed Jamie to find his mum.

Jamie was up early. He could not sleep, he was far too excited. He rushed out and did his rabbit collection quickly, then rushed back for breakfast. He was ready to go, he was so very excited! If he had learnt how to harness the horse and cart, it would have been waiting, ready to go, but he had to wait for Mr Wilson. Eventually they were on their way and then waiting at the station. The train was supposed to arrive at 11:30am and they had a twenty-minute wait. Then, with a great deal of noise and steam, the train arrived. Jamie couldn't see anyone for the steam, then it slowly cleared, and there was his mum with a pram at the end of the platform, where the guard had offloaded the pram and a case. Jamie took off at a run, hugging his mum. He just couldn't stop talking, telling her he had missed her and he loved her.

Mr Wilson came and quietly pulled Jamie off, telling him to bring the case, as he led Mary with the pram out of the station. Mr Wilson put the pram on the cart with Jamie's sister still in it. Jamie struggled with the case as it was heavy, but he wasn't going to let his mum down. He finally got it to the cart. Mr Wilson had got Jamie's mum onto the cart with the pram, which he had now tied down. He picked Jamie up and then the case and put him with his mum. Jamie thought at last as he hugged his mum. Mary leaned down and gently kissed him, then lay back. Jamie looked at her and could see she was very tired. He turned to the baby, who had slept throughout all the noise and bumping about. Jamie thought he looked lovely, all wrapped up in his shawl, with a dummy, then saw that he was awake, looking at him. He fell in love with his little brother, wondering what name Mum had given him. Jamie thought thank goodness it wasn't raining, but the wind was cold. There were some sacks in the box under the seat. He pulled a couple out and put them over his mum to keep her warm.

Jamie sat back until they reached the farm where Mrs Wilson was waiting in the doorway. She greeted his mum, quickly taking Mary inside to the kitchen, getting her seated with a hot bowl of soup with fresh bread while she saw to the baby's comfort. It hadn't taken long for Mr Wilson to unload the cart and wheel the pram and baby into the farm.

Jamie sat and watched as his mum tucked into the soup and bread hungrily, while Mrs Wilson took charge of the baby, who had decided to let everyone know he was there, and hungry too. Mr Wilson asked Mary if she needed anything before he went milking and said that he would take Jamie, to let her get settled, Mary thanked him and said he would be OK for now. Mr Wilson told Jamie to come on, as they were off to the milking sheds.

After a lot of washing of the milking machine parts, the milking pens were made ready for tomorrow's milking and Mr Wilson and Jamie made their way back. Jamie was in a hurry; he wanted to talk and find out about Dad. Where was he and why did he stay behind? He was worried about him.

When they got home, Jamie's mum was nowhere to be seen. Mrs Wilson told Jamie his mother was tired and that she had put her and the baby to bed. She would wake them when they were ready to sit down to dinner. She told Mr Wilson that she had made up their son's room for the time being and that Mary could stay there for the holiday time, if she wanted. He was OK about this, so the rest of the day carried on with Jamie not happy about going to school for the afternoon.

The day went very slowly for Jamie as he wasn't interested, he just wanted to go home to his mum. School finally came to an end and the bell was rung for home time. Jamie ran all the way back to the farm. As soon as he got there, he went into the kitchen: there was Mary, nursing the baby. Jamie stopped, out of breath, then walked slowly over to her, but he was looking at the baby. He asked his mum, 'What is his name?' to which she replied, 'Jamie, his name is Steven.' Then she asked him, 'How are you, son? It's been a long time. We will have to have a long talk later this evening.' 'Where's Dad?' was Jamie's next question. 'Well, Dad is working. He is in the AFS, ready to fight fires, but most evenings, it has all been very quiet. The news said the bombing was on the aerodromes all along the south coast and on the ships in the channel.' Mary explained that Jamie's dad could sleep at the fire station, then go to work from there if called out. They fed him, as well. 'He's OK. I'll tell you more later.'

CHAPTER 11

MARY'S VISIT

It wasn't until the evening time that Mr and Mrs Wilson, with Jamie and Mary, and the two Land Army girls, were able to talk about what had been happening in London. Mary told them there was a very nervous feeling in the air, with the amount of air raid shelters being installed, buildings with their fronts being covered with sandbags, posters telling people what to do in the event of a raid, along with the terribly frightening sound of the sirens. Just scary. But no air raids on London yet. Harry had told Mary to take the baby and go to the farm for a visit. Mary said, 'I have to thank you both, Mr and Mrs Wilson, for your help.' Mr Wilson said, 'It's time you, Mary, called us by our names. My name is Albert, but I'm mostly called Bert, and my wife's name is Cybil. Our son's name is Jack. You will meet him when he gets leave from the army. Please feel at home here. Jamie, you and both you ladies continue as usual. Jamie, you are still our evacuee. OK?'

After supper, Jamie spent the evening talking, telling Mary all about what he had learnt, about the farm, about his rabbit round, and helping on the farm after school. Then he told her he was in the school Christmas play. She would have to come and see it. This went on until the baby began to cry for his feed. Mary kissed Jamie goodnight and Jamie went off to bed.

Mr Wilson told Mary that if there was no rush to get back home to London, she could stay for Christmas. Also, if Mr Monk could get away, he too could come for the holiday period.

CHAPTER 12

CHRISTMAS PLAY 1939

Mary had settled in, using Jack's room, and had accepted Mr and Mrs Wilson's invitation to stay until Christmas was over. Jamie was delighted, as she agreed to see the school play. Mr Wilson had had a long talk with Mary and offered her a job on the farm, if she wanted to stay. He could offer her a place to live. It would not be very grand, but it was watertight and dry. Mary said she would think it over and have a word with Harry. If he thought it was OK, she would let Mr Wilson know.

Jamie was now quite ready for the play, which was to be held on Monday the 18th, a week before Christmas. On the day, the village hall was crowded for the late afternoon play. Jamie was behind the curtains, now dressed in his reindeer costume, including antlers made of wire and covered with wool. There were eight boys of various ages and sizes, of which Jamie was the biggest, now that he was no longer skinny. In the three and a half months he had been living on the farm, he had gained weight and muscle. He was a strong young lad.

Now ready, they were all attached to a kind of rope harness, to a large converted pram, not looking remotely like a sleigh. The play went well; all the children stumbled their way through the nativity. Then came the announcement to the audience that Father Christmas was arriving. The boys all started to pull the sleigh with Santa wedged in it. Very quickly after this, Jamie had his moment of fame. Pulling the sleigh, one of the wheels buckled and started to tip the sleigh over. Jamie, being at the back and the biggest boy, quickly turned around, pulling all the rest of the boys off balance, but managing to hold the sleigh upright enough for Santa to get out with some dignity and untangle the rest of the reindeer, who had fallen into a heap. They all got up and carried on with the play to its end. Everyone was delighted and a great round of applause filled the hall. Christmas had begun.

CHAPTER 13

CHRISTMAS 1939

The next day, on the 19th December 1939, it started to snow. It was going to be a white Christmas, the first in several years. The next day, a letter arrived, addressed to Mary, saying that Harry was free over the Christmas period and asking if he could come to the farm. Send a telegram please. It was a short letter, to the point, but it ended with him telling Jamie he loved him and that he hoped to see him soon. Mary spoke to Cybil, explaining that Harry had asked about coming to the farm.

That afternoon, as they were having a cup of tea, Cybil told Mary to tell Harry to come for Christmas. Mary told Jamie later that day and Jamie went to his money box and gave her half a crown for the telegram, hoping it was enough. Mary started to refuse, telling Jamie it was alright, but Jamie insisted she take it and send his dad the message the next day. This meant going to Chipping Norton's post office. Mrs Wilson told Jamie not to worry; she would take Mary in the buggy as the horse and cart might just get bogged down in the snow. Jamie was happy with that and spent the rest of the day with Mr Wilson, working on the farm, checking everything was OK in the barn and other animal shelters. It snowed on and off all day.

At long last, Jamie was to see his dad. Harry was due to arrive two days later. Mr Wilson told Jamie he was to come with Mr Wilson in the buggy to pick his dad up. As usual these days, the train was running late, causing Jamie to get a little agitated. Mr Wilson told him to calm down; his dad would get there soon. It was just like when his mum arrived. He had to wait for the steam to clear, and then there was his dad. Again, Jamie took off at a run and clung to his dad. Harry lent down and ruffled Jamie's hair and greeted him with, 'Hello, son.' Then he moved up to meet Mr Wilson and they shook hands. Mr Wilson led them to the buggy where they all boarded and started back to the farm.

All the way, Jamie never stopped talking to his dad, filling him in on all the things he did for Mr Wilson.

When they arrived at the farm, waiting at the farm door were Mary and Cybil. As they got down from the buggy, Mary threw her arms around Harry, stepped back, looked at him and said, 'You look tired, luv,' then, almost in the same breath, 'This is Cybil, luv.' Harry shook Cybil's hand as he thanked her for having him there for Christmas.

For Jamie, Christmas had come at last and it would be a perfect day. He wasn't worried about presents, just that they were all together again, and it would be the first Christmas for his brother Steven. His presents for his mum and brother had been ready since he had bought them in Chipping Norton at the market with Mrs Wilson.

Mrs Wilson had bought a scarf for Jamie to give his father, because Jamie had forgotten, in the excitement of his first shopping trip. He thought to himself, I bought all this myself, as sleep overtook him and he drifted into a dreamless night.

The cockerel, called Cock of the Walk by Jamie, woke them all as usual. Jamie lay there for a moment and thought, I never set any traps and I don't have to rush out. It also struck him that it was very cold and, rising and going to the window, he saw there was a heavy frost, mist and snow. The sky was heavy with dark clouds, looking very much like more snow was on its way. It was then he became aware of the smell of bacon.

Jamie got dressed and went down to breakfast. His mum and dad were sitting with Mr and Mrs Wilson, drinking tea. Jamie thought they were up early and tucked into the bacon and eggs Mrs Wilson put in front of him. While eating, he was listening to their conversation, which was mainly about London and what was going to happen if war really started. Jamie spent the rest of the morning with Mary and Steven. Harry had been taken by Mr Wilson for a walk around the farm. Jamie was just itching to give them their Christmas presents, but they would have them later in the afternoon, after the King's speech and dinner.

There were nine of them at the table at 2pm. The table was laden with food, including a leg of pork. Once the pork had been carved and dished out, it was the turn of a chicken, for anyone that preferred it to the pork. On the table were dishes of home-grown vegetables and puddings. The guests were the vicar, Mr Stevens, the teacher, a Mrs Duncan, the Deacon of the church, along with one of the Land Army girls, Jamie and family, and of course Mr and Mrs Wilson. The other Land Army girls had gone home for the holiday period.

The vicar said grace and everyone tucked in. There was also cider to drink and homemade lemonade. The desserts were home-made Christmas pudding, stewed apple and soft fruit pies with custard or cream, then tea or coffee for the adults. By then, Jamie felt ready to bust. It was by far the biggest Christmas dinner Jamie had ever had. They all sat at the table talking, waiting for the Christmas message in the King's speech. The adults toasted the King then spent some time seated around a large fire.

Jamie asked if he could give out the presents under the Christmas tree, which was standing in the corner of the living room. Mrs Wilson said he could. Jamie quickly gave Mary her gift, also Steven's, then gave his dad his present. Then he gave Mrs Wilson her gift for her husband, then Mr Wilson's gift for his wife.

Jamie sat and felt pleased that all those close to him had a gift for Christmas. Shortly afterwards, each of the guests got up and gave Jamie a parcel and wished him a happy Christmas. Now Jamie sat and looked at the parcels and slowly opened one. It was from his mum. It was a knitted balaclava helmet in red wool. Next was the present from Mrs Wilson. She had given him woollen gloves. Mr Wilson's present was a pair of corduroy trousers. It was then that Mr Wilson told Jamie that, in the gun cupboard, was a small rifle and he would teach Jamie how to use it, with his father's permission. Dad's present was a box of water colour paints, with a book and brushes. He also gave permission for Mr Wilson to teach Jamie how to use the rifle safely. Mr Stevens gave Jamie a book on the geography of the world and Mrs Duncan a pencil box with a ruler and pencils. The vicar gave him a bible. Jamie was overwhelmed. All he could say was, 'Thank you to you all and a Merry Christmas!'

Christmas Day was the best Jamie had ever experienced. He slept soundly that night, and never heard the others depart.

Boxing Day was quiet because the weather was now very cold but some of the normal farm work still had to be done. The chickens had to be fed, the horse's stable had to be cleaned and fresh hay given, and above all else, the milking had to be done, as usual.

Just after breakfast, Mr Wilson asked Jamie if any snares had been left out. If so, there may be something in them. What did he think? Jamie thought about it and said, 'I may have left a couple of snares. I should go and check them. It won't take long.' Harry had just come downstairs and heard Jamie say he was going out to have a look at something. Harry said, "What's this about?" and Jamie told him. Harry said that the weather was bad and he felt Jamie shouldn't go out. Jamie said, 'Dad, I have snares out there and if any rabbits were caught, they are dead and will attract foxes, so I must clear them.' Harry looked at his son and saw that he had grown up. He decided to go with Jamie. They put on their overcoats and Jamie led the way. After a short walk, Jamie said, 'There, Dad! See in that one. See how the fox has had a meal? It's half eaten. No good for us, but the farm dog can finish it.'

Later that morning, Harry told Jamie he would be going back to London the next day. Mr Wilson and Jamie went and saw Harry off.

The intervening days between Christmas and the New Year were spent doing as much as possible to get ready for the very bad weather that had been settling in. Already the snow was drifting and making any form of field work extremely difficult. Mary said she was happy that Dad had gone back home before all the snow arrived. Jamie, who was spending his time reading the book he had been gifted, looked up and agreed with her, then went back to his book. Putting the book down, he said, 'Sorry, Mum, I didn't mean to be rude, but yes I am glad Dad got home safely.'

Later that day, Jamie started painting, which seemed to come naturally, however he was going to run out of paper if the weather didn't ease.

Jamie spent most of January at home as the long walk to school was almost impossible with the deep snow. Both Mary and Cybil set about teaching Jamie as much about home life as they could. He was shown how to cook, do general housework, even how to wash and change his brother, Steven. Mr Wilson wasn't very happy about this and said, 'When Jamie is fully grown, he won't need to know all this. He's better off working on the farm and being educated at school.'

It was January 6th and the weather had eased. It was easier to travel. It was then that Mary told Jamie that because of a new system called registration, she would have to go home to London to register the family and get their identity cards. When she returned, she would bring Jamie's card.

The next day, Mr and Mrs Wilson took Jamie and his mum, with Steven, to the station. He saw them off, back to London. Jamie was upset for the rest of the day and very quiet all the way back. Mrs Wilson told Jamie they would be alright and would soon be back.

Several days later, the cold snap returned and Mr Wilson said, 'I think this is going to be a bad winter,' and put the Land Army girls to work cutting wood in the nearby woods for fires in the coming weeks. Very little field work could be done during the rest of January because of the almost continuous snowfall.

January moved on very slowly. Strangely, Jamie had a good time, for he could have some fun in the snow. Both the Land Army girls had snowball fights with Jamie, in which he was the usual target.

Jamie was thinking about Mary and Steven in London and hoping they came back soon. While he waited, he tried to make some skis, but not successfully; they just sank into the snow. Jamie gave that idea up.

CHAPTER 14

LAMBING TIME

It was February and lambing time was about to start. Jamie wondered, why are they born in the cold weather? Mr Wilson said, 'Thank goodness we got the sheep into the shelter as they have started to have their lambs. If you feel well enough, you can wrap up and go and see for yourself.'

Jamie was young, but no fool. He knew Mr Wilson would have him helping, and that would be better than sitting around doing nothing or very little. He would think it over and tell Mr Wilson tomorrow.

At breakfast the next morning, Jamie told Mr Wilson he was coming with him to the lambing barn and he would do as much as he could. He told Mr Wilson he was fed up with his schooling right now and it would be a good change. Then he asked if that was alright with Mrs Wilson. She agreed that he could, for a while.

Lambing always takes place in the early hours, when its dark. Jamie didn't know the first thing about lambing, only that it was very early and very cold when he was woken by Mr Wilson and told to wrap up warm. It was barely 6am, it was still dark, and the cockerel hadn't made its morning crow.

Mr Wilson led Jamie out to the big barn where the sheep had been installed. There were already many newborn lambs being cleaned by the ewes. Jamie was told to watch and learn. Jamie saw one man put his hand into a sheep and pull out the lamb. He wondered what it must have felt like for the ewe. One of the girls called to Mr Wilson that her ewe was in trouble. He called back that he, too, was having a problem. He shouted out instructions: 'Put your hand into the ewe and feel for the head and the two front legs of the lamb. Get the legs out straight, align the head with them and pull the lamb out.'

Somehow, the girl just couldn't do it. She looked at Jamie, shaking her head. Jamie sat for a minute, then got up. He walked over to the man he had watched a little while ago, doing just what Mr Wilson had told the girl to do. He asked him to help. The man nodded and went over to the ewe lying on her side. He lifted her tail, felt under it for the opening and pushed his hand and arm into her. Shortly afterwards, the man eased the new lamb out, then the ewe took over. Then another mess came out! It was then that Jamie felt sick and went to sit down. It was Mr Wilson who came and put his arms around Jamie, saying, 'Watching all this must be very new to you. If you prefer not to watch from now on, you can go back home and to bed?'

Jamie made his way home. That had been quite an experience; one he didn't want to have again!

February moved on with the weather easing in the last week. The thaw set in, faster than Jamie had ever seen it. Tom and the girls were given work on hedging. The thaw finally came to an end and the fields began to empty of the flood water. The weather continued to ease and there were dry days as the month moved on into March.

There was to be another week or so on the farm before the cattle could go outside, now that the fields had dried out. The wind had helped.

Jamie came down for breakfast, ready for school. He went into the living room and found Mrs Wilson crying with happiness. After so many weeks away, Jack was coming home on a short leave.

Work carried on with the farm. Mr Wilson, too, was full of emotion, knowing his son was well.

The next Sunday, they all went to the church hall in the village, where the chaplain held his sermon on his visiting Sundays. Jamie had made himself unavailable by being out in the fields. He never liked church or Sunday school. Mrs Wilson tried to get him to go, but Jamie wouldn't. Perhaps one day he would change his mind. Jamie believed in God, but not in the church, as the priest used God to make you do things. It was so obvious it was for the vicar, not God.

CHAPTER 15

NOT GOOD NEWS

At last, the sun was shining and Jamie had to spend most of the day at school. This wasn't to change for the next couple of months. It would be April before he could spend time on the farm again. The Land Army women were doing most of the work now, along with young Tom.

Jamie was still practising longhand writing, with some help from Mrs Wilson, in the evenings. He was getting better, slowly. He would learn scriptwriting.

March was moving on. There was very little news about the war. What there was was mainly through talk in the village, also from the traitor, Lord Haw-Haw, on the radio. He was saying there was bombing in the channel where Germany were sinking the cargo boats; but the radio said they were missing the boats mostly. Mr Wilson said, 'I don't think their bombing is any good, thank goodness, but until they get better, we just carry on with the farming and you with your schooling. So off with you to school.'

It was three weeks before Jack came home on leave for a few days. Mr and Mrs Wilson sat and talked with him for a long time. Later, he made friends with Jamie but wouldn't tell him about the army or where he had been, or what was happening. Jamie wanted to know, but he didn't learn until a considerable time later.

CHAPTER 16

SPRING

It had been a very long and cold winter, but in April, the spring weather came in sunny, warm and bright, with showers. This caused the trees and hedgerows to spring into action. Everywhere the fields were turning refreshingly green. The corn and barley had sprouted and were growing fast. Mr Wilson was pleased there had been a good number of lambs born this year. The year looked promising. The sow had farrowed and now had eight piglets chasing her around, always hungry.

On a day when Jamie had little to do, he went to the spring and cleared some of the stones, making a clearer channel for the pig's wallow. He was nearly finished with the wallow and was beginning to leave when as he turned to move out, he stepped on one of the rounded stones, slipped and fell. As he fell, he turned and his shoulder smashed onto the stones. There was a loud crack. Jamie rolled onto his back and screamed in pain. Lying across the round stone left him in constant pain. He was there a considerable length of time.

Young Tom came to have a look to see if Jamie was doing OK with the wallow and found Jamie lying there. Tom quickly ran to the farm, about half a mile away, and told Mr Wilson that Jamie was injured and needed help. The village doctor was sent for. He arrived as they were about to take the buggy out onto the field leading to the wallow. They all quickly made their way there.

Jamie had not been able to move and looked in a bad way. The doctor examined Jamie, saying to Mr Wilson, 'He has broken his collar bone.' He needed hospitalisation.

Tom was sent back to the farm to bring over the flatbed wagon which would be more comfortable to move Jamie on, back to the farm, along the main road. There they could meet the ambulance to take Jamie to the Oxford infirmary.

Jamie was only in hospital for the rest of the day and one night, then he was told that he could go home.

It was the next day that Mr Wilson arrived with the buggy to take Jamie back, with his arm in a sling and his hand on his shoulder, and the instruction that that was the way he should wear it for the next six weeks. No working.

Back at the farm, they found Mrs Wilson waiting. She led Jamie into the kitchen where she made him sit down to tea and cake, all the time telling Jamie, looking stern, that there was to be no more working until the shoulder had mended. Though Jack had gone back to his barracks after his week's leave, Jamie felt Mr Wilson was no longer as attentive as before, and wondered if he had done something wrong. Jamie had lost his rabbit round, as that had gone to Tom. Jamie just had school, but he wasn't happy. He missed working on the farm; it was far more interesting.

CHAPTER 17

SPRING 1940

April gave way to May. Summer was on its way. It was looking like it was going to be a very good harvest. The weather was warm, dry and sunny, with very occasional showers. 'Nothing to damage the crop,' Mr Wilson was heard saying to the Land Army girls.

Most afternoons, Jamie was away from school and lazing in the fields, which he revelled in. One weekend, he was not working, sitting in the shade of a large oak when he suddenly felt lonely and homesick. He was longing for the old familiar London streets. He wondered how his friends at home were doing. He would like to see them, perhaps for a game of football, just the way they used to, using the church door as a goal. Jamie heard the Land Army girls talking about ships being attacked on the way to England from America. That, apparently, was where the war was being fought. Jamie thought, why is this happening? Didn't England rule the waves? It was now that the news came filtering through via gossip that there was big trouble in a place called France. France had been attacked by Germany and the English army was helping the French army to stop them. That was the village talk. Mr Wilson told Jamie, 'It's only talk, lad. Nothing has been said officially. Until it is, we just get on with our work. OK?'

The weather stayed hot and dry. The corn was showing good, full ears. In three months it would be ready for harvest. Jamie loved that time. It would be hot, dusty, and he would probably be stacking stooks.

It was May, so Mr Wilson started the haymaking. This would be the cattle fodder for next winter. They made several hay ricks from the grass that was eventually mown. Jamie watched the loading on the high-sided wagon. He should be helping with unloading the wagons, making the ricks and putting some into the barns. Between school and reading, Jamie hardly noticed time passing or that he hadn't heard from his mum for a long time.

The lanes were not so quiet. Lorries with big red crosses on their sides, loaded with soldiers, were moving into the country. Both Mrs Wilson and Jamie stopped and stood aside while the lorries went by. Some of the soldiers in the back wore bandages which looked bloody. Mrs Wilson shook her head and said, 'War!'

Planes were flying overhead. Jamie watched as they flew very low, making that lovely engine sound. These were English Hurricanes and Spitfires, fighter planes. The engines made such unmistakable sounds, much loved by many.

Gradually the month moved on into June. Still very dry, sunny days. It was looking very much like summer had set in. Jamie spent much of his free time just lazing about in the meadow, watching the clear blue sky for any signs of aeroplanes, until someone called his name to snap him back to reality.

CHAPTER 18

NOT GOOD NEWS

BBC broadcast said that many of our airfields, Biggin hill, Mansfield and Tangmere, in the south of England, had been bombed and that there had been many casualties. The newscaster passed the opinion that the German Luft Waffer was attacking our airfields, trying to cripple the RAF. Somehow, the RAF kept fighter planes in the air, attacking their bombers. Mr Wilson told Jamie, 'We can only hope and pray that the Germans don't succeed in hurting our RAF.' Mr Wilson then said, 'Jamie, now your shoulder is better, you'll be able to do light work after school. You can help me, as we still have a farm to work. Because the food shortages are getting bad, we need to grow more. Soon there will be some form of rationing in England, which will be hard on everyone.'

On the 6pm news, it was revealed that the city of Paris had fallen to the German army. This came as terrible news to England. Now invasion was the talk everywhere. 'Are the Germans coming?' Jamie asked Mr Wilson, and 'What do we do?' Mr Wilson answered, 'Nothing, son. We just do our work here until things change.'

That evening, Jamie was sitting on the stairs, as he couldn't sleep. He heard Mrs Wilson say, 'God I hope our Jack's alright. We haven't heard.' Mr Wilson said, 'The army will tell us soon enough dear, don't worry.'

Jamie went to bed and slept fitfully.

CHAPTER 19

TASTE OF WAR

Every day at school, at playtime in the school playground, Jamie sat on a wall and watched as the fighter planes roared past, heading south east towards the attacking German bombers. He would love to fly in one of those beautiful machines. It was a dream that, later in life, might just happen. Occasionally, in the night, he thought there were aircraft flying over the farm. As nothing happened, and the droning sound faded away, he would lie awake for a while, then drift back to sleep. Telling Mrs Wilson about this, he felt some relief and was no longer frightened. Mrs Wilson knew he was troubled as he hadn't slept very well. Also he had not had any mail for several weeks from Mary, his mother, even though he had been writing to her. Mrs Wilson decided to keep an eye on Jamie and write to Mary.

Summertime was now in operation. There was daylight until 8pm. Later, another hour would be added and there would be daylight until 10pm. The nights would be shorter. During this time, the days would be full of work, due to the darkening evening. Then it would be hurry home for supper, a hot bath and a good night's rest.

Every Friday, while the workers were having their lunch, Mr Wilson would come to wherever they were resting and pay them for their week's work. Mr Wilson had a special packet for Jamie. It was his first ever wage. Jamie opened it, wondering what he would find. What he found was fifteen shillings. Jamie's first thought was for his mum. He made sure that as soon as he got home, ten shillings were put in his money box to give to his mother the next time she visited. He hoped his mother would visit soon as he had been thinking about her every night and dreaming about seeing her and the rest of the family. The remaining five shillings was his, and he wondered just what to do with it. Jamie had little idea about money. Mrs Wilson had been with him when he had first had money, but the Christmas shopping had been his only experience. Now he had money but didn't know what to do with it. He would have to save it or give it to his mum. Jamie was sure that he would be advised on how best to use the money he was saving by Mrs Wilson or his mum.

The summer that had shown promise seemed to have settled in as it moved on into July and double summertime. The German army never came but the war hadn't finished; it was still there. Every day, Jamie would see the Spitfires or Hurricanes flying across the sky. Sometimes they looked to be treetop height as they flew across the farm fields. At this height, Jamie could see the detail and sometimes even the pilot.

On one occasion, a Spitfire moved its wings up and down in a kind of wave to Jamie. He hoped and prayed that one day he would fly in one of those lovely machines. At night, Jamie could hear aeroplanes going over the village with a much heavier engine sound. He thought there were probably German bombers, but they were heading in the wrong direction. They were going north west over the farm and he had no idea what was in that direction. Jamie didn't know very much about the layout of English towns.

CHAPTER 20

WAR COMES CLOSER

June moved into July and with double summertime, the days stayed bright and sunny until 10pm. The month promised to remain bright and sunny and very dry. Crops were golden and it would not be long before they were ready for harvesting. Mr Wilson said, 'Jamie, the harvest will begin next week, in July. This will take us into August, provided this weather holds. I understand that the schools will be releasing you children to work in the fields during harvest. In the mornings you will attend school for lessons.' Jamie changed the subject and said, 'Mr Wilson, there have been a lot of lorries driving along the Oxford road. I can't see who's in them, but I think it's soldiers.' Mr Wilson replied, 'It is probably because now the services must be enlisting as many men as possible into the forces. Jamie, when you're old enough, you could be called into the army, if we are still at war. I think some of those are going to a camp somewhere near here in the countryside. There must be an army camp not far from Oxford. There is also an RAF station somewhere near, as well, as we see far more aeroplanes flying around here these days. Things are beginning to look better for England.'

Jamie learnt from the radio evening news that on June 14th, France had surrendered. Mr and Mrs Wilson were shocked at the news. It had taken a couple of weeks for the world to be told. The radio reported that the German and British armies had been engaged in a desperate battle. Now the bombers were hitting the north of England as well as the south. Mr Wilson thought those in the north must be coming from Norway. This aroused Jamie's interest. Where was and what was Norway? Was it part of the German country? This was new geography for him; something that Mr Stevens had not spoken about in geography lessons.

It was up to Mr Wilson to explain that Norway was a country over the seas, to the east of England, and that as far as they knew, it had been conquered by Germany, therefore they were able to fly aeroplanes from there over to the north of England. Jamie heard from the newscaster that many of the bombers had attacked the RAF stations in the north east, in the same way they had attacked in the south, but the RAF had continued to attack the bombers as normal. The bombers, trying to return, had been met and engaged by the RAF, who shot down many of them.

The weather was still dry and sunny. Wildlife was everywhere: the fields were alive with rabbits; lots of young kits running about. Jamie had seen several hawks making kills.

CHAPTER 21

A WILDLIFE INTRUDER

As usual, one morning, Jamie set out for school. As he was approaching the farm, he became aware of a lot of noise coming from the direction of the henhouse. As he reached the yard gate, there was the sound of a gunshot. What was this all about, Jamie wondered.

He reached the farm and found Mr Wilson with a shotgun in hand, standing in front of the henhouse. It looked like a slaughter-house. There were dead chickens lying around in the scratching yard, also one very dead fox; somehow the fox had managed to get into the henhouse and run amuck, killing the hens. Given the chance, he would try to take them to his den. Jamie asked Mr Wilson what would happen to the dead chickens. Mr Wilson politely replied, 'Son, they'll go into the farm's cold store, then perhaps in due time we can have some for lunch, you never know. We didn't slaughter them, and they are not on my allocation, so we can eat them without referring them to the department of AG. & Fish.'

Jamie nodded, said, 'Bye' and carried on to school. He wasn't really interested in school these days, he just wanted to see his mum.

The evening news reported that heavy raids had taken place on the airfields and that a great deal of damage had been done, making it difficult for some airfields. It was also reported that bombing raids had taken place on other airfields along the south coast.

Jamie continued with school every morning, then every after-noon, after dinner, in the fields with the harvesting.

CHAPTER 22

HARVEST

June moved into July 1940 and the weather was still bright, sunny and hot. The harvest was coming in quickly; the reaper was making excellent time. The children, alongside the farmhands, were doing well. The stooks were standing and would dry out over the next week, ready for the thresher. The corn heads were full and ripe. There should be good crop. Mr Wilson said that it was looking good and the farm would meet the target asked for by AG. & Fish. There was big demand in the major towns and cities as a great deal of food from overseas just wasn't getting to England because of the shipping losses at sea.

While having his bath that evening, Jamie asked Mrs Wilson if there was any news from his mother. Mrs Wilson told him, 'Nothing so far, Jamie. Maybe soon.'

That night, Jamie was restless, dreaming about home, playing with his mates in the streets again. It was nice, being here on the farm, but he missed the streets of London. He was in the playground and as the game ended, in his dream, he was awakened by the sound of the cockerel crowing to the sunrise. Jamie sat up and quickly realised he was late; sunrise! He should have been up and out and on his rabbit round, then on his way to school at the break of dawn.

He sat for a short while then went down to breakfast. Mrs Wilson asked him if he was well, as he was late down. Jamie answered, 'Yes, just overslept.' He quickly finished and set off for school. Someone else would do the rabbit round. But he just dawdled and finally sat down on an old tree stump and said out loud, 'Blow school! I am not going. I'll stay here and watch the animals for a change.'

Jamie was sitting on the side of the Oxford road, gazing into space. Presently he became aware of someone coming down the road dressed in khaki, walking with a slight limp. As he drew nearer, he saw it was Jack.

Jamie ran to him to see that Jack had been injured, sometime recently. There was a nasty-looking red scar down the side of his face. They both stopped and Jack said, 'Hello, young Jamie.' Jamie replied, 'Hello, Jack. Mum and Dad will be delighted to see you!' Jack said, 'Come on, we'll walk in together.'

When they got to the farm, Mrs Wilson came rushing out and threw her arms around Jack, hugging him and crying at the same time. Turning to Jamie, she said, 'Jamie, get Dad.'

Jamie was off like a shot to the harvest field where he found Mr Wilson. Breathless, Jamie told him that Jack was at home. Mr Wilson said, 'Stay here, son, for a little while. See everything is OK, then make your way home. I'm off home.'

It was at dinner that evening that Jamie could talk to Jack.

CHAPTER 23

JACK'S STORY

It was after the evening dinner that Mr and Mrs Wilson allowed Jamie to sit up and hear what Jack had to tell them.

Jack started by saying, 'When Paris fell and Germany had invaded France and Holland had surrendered, our forces were in a trap, and were being pushed back towards the coast. As my platoon tried to use the roads, we found them crowded with refugees, fleeing from the German army. We just had to push on in our lorries by pushing our way through the refugees. We knew that the German aircraft would start strafing the road, as they would need them clear for their armoured units to push us faster. The strafing of the road killed hundreds of the refugees. The surviving refugees soon learnt that, at the sound of an aeroplane, they were to get off the road and into the ditches. Soon all our lorries were damaged or on fire and we had to dump them and spoil their engines. We couldn't leave them for the German army to use. As we made our way towards the coast, my platoon lost men and we had to carry the wounded. From then on, it was a long slog toward our lines. There were skirmishes with German advanced patrols. We destroyed a small bridge as we marched. After several days, we reached the outskirts of our own force's front line. There we stopped and were given food and water. A sergeant told us to push on to the coast. He directed us to the town of Dunkirk. It was seething with French civilians, French soldiers and our troops. There were thousands of us in this small town and the troops spilled over onto the beach. All the time, the German bombers were divebombing the beach and the town. There was hot metal flying everywhere, shrapnel causing a terrible amount of injuries. My mates and I got ourselves onto the beach and came under the orders of a beachmaster.

At night, we tried to get some sleep, but the bombers denied us that pleasure. In the mornings, we joined the lines of men, standing up to our necks in the sea, hoping to be picked up and taken to a naval ship standing offshore, but no luck there. In the night, I went to what was called The Moll. It was there I copped these wounds. There were pieces of shrapnel in my leg as another ripped up the side of my face. I woke up on the beach with my mates. My leg was bandaged with field dressings as well as my face. Next morning, two of my mates half carried me to the Moll. I managed, with their help, to board a small boat that took us to a destroyer. Luckily, this one made it back home. I was taken past here some time ago in an army ambulance, to an army hospital. Once I was able to walk almost normally, I was given leave for two weeks, but must report back when I am fully fit for duty. Well, Mum, I made my way home. Mum, Dad, that's what has been going on since May. Several thousand men were rescued but nearly all were wounded and thousands were left behind. I thank God for my mates. I came home and have spent all this time in the army hospital.'

Mrs Wilson quietly got up and went to the kitchen, to make a pot of tea, while Mr Wilson went to a cupboard and got out a bottle of whisky, then sent Jamie to bed.

CHAPTER 24

BACK TO NORMAL

Jack spent the rest of his leave under his mother's care. Mrs Wilson made sure he relaxed while she, herself, got used to Jack's new face, with his terrible scar. She was making sure he was well fed before he had to go to war once more.

Mr Wilson spent time with Jack every evening and weekend. Unfortunately, he still had to carry on with the farm work as it never, never stopped.

Jamie was pushed a little bit into the background, but his curiosity made him ask a lot of questions of Jack, about the Dunkirk beaches and how he had been rescued. Jack would not elaborate on anything he had already said to his mother, father and Jamie. He would not tell Jamie anything more, as Jamie was a bit too young.

Jamie, although he wanted to stay at home and talk with Jack, was made to go to school in the normal way. Being a boy, he had to tell the other boys what Jack had told him. The teachers tried to stop him; they felt that the children were too young to hear this news, but children will be children.

In the afternoons, Jamie was back working in the fields. This would go on the whole time that the harvest was being gathered in and the weather stayed fair.

Jamie, like many other children, would spend the rest of the summer working, until the harvest was complete.

Near the end of July, Jack's leave ended and he said his good-byes to Mrs Wilson, who was in tears. Mr Wilson helped Jack onto the buggy, then drove off with him.

Jamie stood and watched and wondered if he would ever see Jack again.

Jamie was still struggling with his arithmetic and English but worst of all was his spelling. He needed better schooling, but it would be a considerable amount of time before that would happen.

As the harvest was almost finished, Jamie knew that soon there would be only school, all day.

CHAPTER 25

AUTUMN 1940

August had started as the harvest was coming to an end. The quiet period of the year on the farm began; a time when repairing hedges and fencing had to be done, as well as checking that the barns and sheds were all secure, checking machinery and servicing them. Also the collection of any hedgerow berries and fruit. It was a month that passed all too quickly and soon it was September.

The war news was not good. At the end of the first week, German bombers had started bombing London. Over the next week it was continuous, day and night, causing a lot of damage and casualties. It was destined to last and become known as the Blitz on London. In the dusk, looking towards London from the farm, in the darkening sky, a red glow of fire could be seen over London. This was a clear reminder of the terrible price London was paying.

On the 15th, at breakfast, there were three small presents on the table for Jamie and cards wishing him a happy birthday. On opening the present from Mary and Harry, Jamie saw that it contained a woollen jumper from his mum and a book about King Arthur and the knights of the round table. From both Mr and Mrs Wilson were items of practical clothing. Mrs Wilson gave Jamie some new trousers, and Mr Wilson, new boots. Jamie was well pleased with these, as winter was on its way and he needed them. Mrs Wilson had made a birthday cake with only a little icing, but no candles.

Very little changed, either at school or on the farm, over the next three weeks. September was coming to an end and the weather changed. It became cold and with heavy rainfall. Most of the trees were either losing their leaves or had already shed them.

A chill was in the air. Jamie asked Mr Wilson about work for him to do, as soon it would be winter. Mr Wilson Told Jamie that the work would be there regardless of the season and not to worry, as he would be asked in due time. For now, Jamie was to get on with his schooling

CHAPTER 26

GOOD NEWS

Jamie was listening to the radio news. It was announced that, on the evening of the 7th September, the first raids had been carried out over the London dock area. There had been much damage all around the docks and casualties were high. Hearing this news, Jamie spoke to Mrs Wilson, asking if she thought his mum and dad would be alright. She told Jamie she thought they probably were.

That night, Jamie sat and wrote a letter to his mum. It was several days later that a letter arrived, addressed to Mr and Mrs Wilson. When Jamie came home from school that afternoon, Mrs Wilson called Jamie into the kitchen and told him to sit down as she had received a letter and she would read it to him. With a worried frown, Jamie did as he was told. Mrs Wilson sat and read out the letter to Jamie, which told him that his mum and dad were in a bit of trouble. The house had been damaged and a bomb had made it impossible to stay there anymore. All were safe, but now they were homeless and Mary had asked if there was anywhere they could stay locally, as they were temporarily staying with her mum and dad. Jamie asked, 'Can they stay here?' Mrs Wilson said that maybe they could find a place, as Mary and Harry were due to come in a couple of days for a visit. Jamie jumped for joy and excitedly started talking about seeing them. Mrs Wilson said, 'Go and have your wash, ready for dinner.' As he left, she had a worried look on her face. Where, oh where, would they stay?

CHAPTER 27

THE FORGE

Mrs Wilson, after thinking for a while, asked her husband if the old smithy cottage close to the Banbury road was still there, and could it be made liveable? Mr Wilson replied, 'I'll have a look at it and see what we can do. Mary will have to consider whether she would stay there.'

The next day, Mr Wilson looked over the smithy cottage. It could be made into a good, liveable space, but it would need some hard work.

A couple of days later, Mary arrived with baby and was settled in Jack's room for her stay.

That evening, at dinner, Mary explained that, in London, the air raids had been happening every evening for a week. It was decidedly bad and looked as if it was set to continue for a lot longer.

Early the next morning Harry arrived. He had hitchhiked from London and walked to the farm. They spoke for some time at breakfast about the possible place to stay. Mary was interested and so later that morning, Mr Wilson took Mary and Harry on the buggy across the fields to where the smithy stood.

Mary saw a thatched cottage, looking a bit rundown, but with appeal. They all went into the cottage, through a door which was quite small in height. There was a wonky porch over the entrance. The plant around the porch was in flower, with one red clematis flower. It looked like it had run wild.

Once inside, Mary had a good look at all the rooms. The kitchen was quite large, with flagstone flooring. There was an iron range that needed cleaning and blacking. Hanging up along one wall there were numerous kitchen tools. There was a large wooden table in the middle of the kitchen that looked pretty good but would need a good scrubbing. There was a large washing copper with a fireplace beneath. This was brick built and big enough for large families' washing, or even a bath for youngsters.

Moving on into the living room, it was quite spacious. The front door led out to a very large garden. There was also another door in one of the walls. When opened, it led to a narrow stair-case. The upper rooms were bedrooms. There were three large bedrooms and one small. Another short stairway lead to the loft area, which covered the length of the cottage.

Back in the kitchen, Harry had found another door leading to an outhouse that led to the rear garden, in which the outside toilet was situated. This he talked to Mary about. They looked at the toilet and saw that it was very primitive, very dirty.

Mary continued to look at the living areas in the cottage. The curtains were no longer any good; they would have to be replaced. All the floors were laid with flagstones, which would make it cold. Something would need to be done there.

Turning to Mr Wilson, Mary said, 'Mr Wilson, if we take this place, which I think we will, can I bring my friends and neighbours, who are in the same position we are? The reason I'm leaving London is that the bombing that has destroyed our home is contin-uous. Some people are calling it the Blitz and saying that Germany is concentrating on London in preparation for an invasion of England.' Mr Wilson said, 'Yes, you can bring as many friends or family that can be supported in the forge cottage. Are you staying, Harry?' Harry answered, 'No, I am in the fire service and must get back to duty.' Mary said, 'In that case, Mr Wilson, I would be delighted to take this cottage to live in. Thank you so much.'

They all returned to the buggy and Mr Wilson drove them back to the farm, where they had midday lunch. Now Mrs Wilson and Mr Wilson asked if Mary would like to work for the farm, as this would help her financially. They weren't thinking of renting the forge cottage, but it would be part of her employment. If she did work for the farm, she could be registered as a farm hand, and living there would help.

Mary said, 'Yes, I would like to do that, but I must first speak with Harry, who will be going back to London. I don't think there will be any problem.'

Mr Wilson told Mary that the forge cottage had been empty for several years. The smithy had been an old man and he had passed away. His son was going to take over as blacksmith, but he was called up for the army. He was sent abroad, and they hadn't heard from him since.

Later, at dinner, they told Jamie that his mum was going to stay and work on the farm, but not his dad, who would be going back to London in the morning. His mum would be living in the forge cottage. Jamie had only seen the forge building from across the fields. He had never been there, but soon he would go there for a look. Jamie was very happy that his mum would be there.

CHAPTER 28

REFUGEES

Now that Mary had been given a place to live and permission to have friends and family from London come and stay, the next thing to do was let them know.

The next day, Mrs Wilson took Mary to Chipping Norton post office, where Mary spent two shillings of her precious money sending a telegram to her friend, Alice, to tell Lillian, Mary's sister, that there was a place for them, away from London. They then returned to the farm, where Mary began packing her belongings, ready to move into the forge cottage, to get it ready for herself and the expected new arrivals.

Four days later, after Mary had worked hard and Mr Wilson had sent the Land Army girls over for a short time to help her, the cottage looked much improved, but there was still a lot of work to do before Mary could call it home.

It was three days later that Lillian, with her seven-year-old daughter Kathleen, arrived. Shortly afterwards, Mary's friend, Alice, along with her five-year-old son Kenny, arrived. Both were pulling heavily-laden prams filled with clothing, bedding, food, hopping equipment and personal items.

On their arrival, they were pretty exhausted. Pushing and pulling the prams had made them tired. Coming into the cottage, they flopped into any seat available, or just sat on the floor. Lillian said, 'Mary, put the kettle on, be a luv. I'm gasping.'

Once Mary had brought in sandwiches and a pot of tea, they started to tell Mary all that had been happening in London, and how glad they were to be out of it. Although they were safe, their husbands had had to stay behind for work. They knew they would worry but could do little about it.

After a little while they went upstairs with Mary and the bedrooms were agreed upon. Once this was done, each of the new arrivals set to and unpacked the prams.

Next morning, after breakfast, Mary explained the offer Mr Wilson had proposed, for the women to sign on as farmhands for the duration of their stay. They considered this and by the end of breakfast, agreed to do just that. It would bring in a wage for each of them so that they could support themselves.

They worked all day, cleaning the cottage. In the late morning, a wagon arrived at the cottage, stacked with armchairs and a sofa, a table and chairs. There was also a box with a large variety of cutlery. The curtain material needed adjusting to fit the small cottage windows. Mary, speaking to Jamie, said that it was getting cold. Jamie said, 'Mum, you must get lots of wood in, as the nights are getting longer and will be getting much colder. Mum, I ain't been here long, but it gets very cold. Ask Mr Wilson what to do.'

The next day, Mr Wilson spoke to the women and gave them a list of things they would need, then, in the afternoon, took Mary and Alice into Chipping Norton to buy lanterns, oil, candles, a torchlight with batteries and some coarse matting for the floors. There were things the women wanted as well, like woollens and wellies, and on Mr Wilson's suggestion, raincoats and other gear. All this, Mr Wilson paid for, then told them he would take a little off their wages each week to cover it.

They were much happier in their outlook for the winter months that were not far off.

CHAPTER 29

JAMIE MOVES

Jamie asked Mrs Wilson and Mr Wilson if he could now stay with his mum. Mr Wilson would have a talk with the authorities to discuss the situation and talk to Mary.

That night, Mr Wilson said there was no problem with the authorities, concerning Jamie's request to live with his mother. It was decided that Jamie would choose when he came home from school that afternoon.

Mr Wilson, Mrs Wilson and Mary sat together in the farm living room and asked Jamie what he would like to do: carry on living with Mr and Mrs Wilson or move to the forge and live with his mother. Jamie told Mr and Mrs Wilson that he loved them very much, but if they didn't mind, he would like to stay with his mum. Nobody objected and they helped Jamie pack his old, battered suitcase, then Mr Wilson took him over to the forge and settled him in.

Jamie felt a bit torn between his mother and Mr and Mrs Wilson, who had taught him so much during his time on the farm. He had told Mr Wilson he still wanted to work on the farm on the afternoons that he was away from school. Jamie had no idea that, because his situation had changed, he was no longer an evacuee. Now he was considered a refugee. He had no permanent address and nowhere to live, except at temporary addresses.

Mary had to go to Chipping Norton town hall to register Jamie as living with her as her son. As usual, there were paperwork problems and it took most of the afternoon for Mary to get it sorted out. Now Jamie was considered returned family. All allowances as an evacuee were terminated and Mary now had to look after him herself.

The weather all that month had been hot dry and the harvest had been brought in. Mr Wilson was extremely pleased with the harvest. It would be very profitable this year and now the fields would lie fallow until next year. But that wasn't the completion of farming for the year; now the Land Army girls had help from Alice, Lillian and Mary, all working on the farm. All three had been shown how to milk cows, herd them and look after the other animals of the farm, such as the chickens and horses, who had to be mucked out daily. Then, in the evening, they made dinner for themselves and the three children for when they returned from school.

Jamie still carried on setting some snares during the evening time, hoping to catch rabbits. In the past, anything that was caught in his snares had to be given to Mr Wilson, but now Jamie could keep them or give them to his mother. Mrs Wilson had also taught Jamie to pick mushrooms in the early hours of the morning. This he continued to do most mornings, and these he could give to Mary. Mary thought it was far too early in the morning for a young lad like Jamie to be traipsing across the fields in the early morning dew, but Jamie was used to it and took no notice. He very often brought home a bag of mushrooms, freshly picked, and a couple of rabbits and gave them to Mary.

Mary had to do something that she had never done before: she had to learn to skin and clean a rabbit, ready for cooking and eating. She felt that she was learning a great deal more about life than she had ever done before.

The rest of the catch went to the farm.

CHAPTER 30

JAMIE'S DAD

A letter arrived for Mary. As she opened it, Jamie was watching her and saw her go pale. He quickly asked, 'Mum, what's wrong?' Mary sat quietly for a few minutes, then said, 'Jamie, I am going to London. Something has happened to Dad and he is in hospital. He's been hurt by a falling wall from a burning factory. I must go and see how he is. I'll go tomorrow, if I can get away, and try to get back before Christmas.'

Jamie wanted to go as well, but Mary said, 'No, Jamie. Stay here, I'll go alone. I'll let you know as quickly as possible how Dad is.'

Mary told the others that she would be leaving for London tomorrow. Harry had been injured and she needed to see how he was.

Next day, Mary went to the station for the train to London.

Aunt Alice also received a letter. It had a foreign-looking stamp on it and looked as though it had had a lot of problems getting to her. She took the letter out into the kitchen and sat and read it. She looked quite happy when she returned it. The letter was to tell her that her husband was in the desert. It was hard going but he was well and thought he should let her know. What Alice didn't like about the letter was that it had been heavily censored. There must have been a lot more written than she was allowed to see.

Things settled into a routine and remained that way until Mary returned. Jamie had spoken to Mr Wilson about his dad and said that Mary was in London for a short while. He also said he was wondering about Christmas, as things were not all that good now that they didn't have any stores. Jamie had not been able to catch any game and their store was practically empty. Mr Wilson told him not to worry; he would see that there was something on the table for the family on Christmas Day.

Mary came back ten days later. She told Jamie that Harry had had his legs badly burned from his clothing catching fire. It was going to be a few weeks before he would be able to walk, then he was to be discharged from hospital and also the auxiliary fire service. When he was discharged, he would like to come and stay with Mary and Jamie for a while.

CHAPTER 31

CHRISTMAS EVE 1940

Work went on on the farm until 4pm Christmas Eve when everybody finished and went home. They immediately set about putting up decorations to show that it was Christmas. Jamie helped make things like holly bowers and mistletoe, which he had found in the wood and had climbed to get, also laurel leaves. There were no paper chains, because of the shortage of paper, to make it feel like Christmas.

Jamie went out into the woods, along with Kenny. They cut a small fir tree sapling down and dragged it into the house. This was now their Christmas tree. There were no lights or anything to put on it. No tinsel, angel or star. Not this year. But it looked like a Christmas tree.

When they returned, there was a surprise, as three soldiers were standing in the doorway: Jamie's uncles, Harold and Albert, and their friend, Frank. A light snack was made for them, which was a plate of homemade chips, an egg and bread.

Shortly after dinner, Jamie and the other two children were sent to bed.

Each of the women had done some shopping over the past few weeks in town, making sure their kids would have something in their stockings. It was an austere time, but it was Christmas.

Jamie wasn't expecting anything for himself; he was just content that the family was all there, with good friends.

Christmas Eve morning had dawned overcast, with dull, grey clouds and a cold wind blowing hard, but there had been no sound of aircraft overnight. Jamie overslept for the first time in ages. Getting dressed as quickly as he could, he ran downstairs to the kitchen to get the fire going, as it was not only cold, but Mary would want to start making breakfast. For that, she would need a good fire going in the grate.

Jamie started the fire and got it going before Mary came down. The room was beginning to warm up. Christmas began to look just a little bit better with a nice fire.

Jamie knew everybody was going to be busy. He had checked the cold store and it was virtually empty. They would have to make do with all that they had. Breakfast was porridge, with some honey to sweeten it, or bread and marge.

Late that afternoon, Mr and Mrs Wilson and the two Land Army girls came over. Mrs Wilson talked with Mary and unpacked two chickens, and a small bit of pork. Jamie heard his name and the mention of his store and what he had collected, but he could not hear clearly what was said.

Mr Wilson spent some time with the three men in uniform. Jamie wondered what they talked about.

Mary made Jamie do the washing up to get him out of the way. Jamie didn't mind, as it would be Christmas Day tomorrow. He wished his dad could be there.

Jamie made his way to bed and saw that Mrs Wilson had brought some homemade wine and all the adults were sitting and having a drink, catching up with the news.

That night, Jamie slept well, but didn't forget his pillow case, just in case Santa came.

CHAPTER 32

CHRISTMAS DAY 1940

Christmas Day dawned dull and grey with a cold wind still blowing hard, but Jamie had awakened early and, looking at the pillow case at the bottom of the bed, saw that Santa had been. There was only the one present, which was going to come in very handy. It was a jack knife he could hook onto his belt. Great, he thought, it's going to be very useful, and thank you!

With no more ado, Jamie got up, went downstairs and started the fire, ready for his mum. It was then he heard the laughter and cries of joy from the other kids and knew Santa had visited them as well.

Breakfast was done with as soon as possible; still porridge and honey, which was now getting low. There was a lot of work to be finished before Christmas dinner at 3pm, in time for the King's speech, if the radio battery was OK.

The three women had set to preparing the chicken, vegetables and getting the piece of pork soaking in some kind of herbal liquid, ready for boxing day. The kitchen, with Mary, Alice, Lillian and young Kathy all working there, was overcrowded.

Jamie left, taking Kenny with him. Jamie knew that if he stayed, they would have him peeling potatoes. He remembered harvesting spuds and how he had wished never to see one again, but he liked to eat them, so would leave them to the others to deal with.

Now the weather had cleared, with some weak sunshine, but it was still very cold. Jamie went to see the three men, who were sitting by the fire around the table chatting, while having a game of cards. Jamie sat and listened as they all talked about the war and the army and the bombing on London.

At 2:30pm, the dinner was ready, with roast chicken, roast potatoes, kale, Brussels sprouts, parsnips and even a Yorkshire pudding to help fill everybody. The dessert was a mixture of pre-served fruit and custard. They listened to the King's speech, then drank a toast to the King and victory and to the end of war.

Jamie got Kenny to lie on his bed and within a few minutes, he was asleep. Jamie just sat there and wondered what the New Year would bring, before closing his eyes in sleep.

Boxing Day dawned much like Christmas morning, with a cold wind and dull skies, until late morning when the skies cleared and the sun shone again; not very warm, but bright. Mary, Alice and Lillian prepared the pork dinner. It was at the dinner table that Harold, Albert and Frank announced that they would have to leave that afternoon and report back to their units. Unbeknown to Jamie, this was to be the last time he would see any of them for several years. At 4pm, he gave a cheery wave as they left.

The next day, the farm was back in full swing. There would be no more holidays until Easter.

There was a heavy air raid on London on the 29th.

It was two weeks later that Mary left for London. On her way to the hospital, a letter had arrived, telling Mary that Harry was to be discharged in the next few days.

Mary collected Harry and thanked the hospital staff for their help in making Harry better, then they made their way to the station and started back to the forge.

Mr Wilson had arranged with Mary that he would be at the station to help Harry.

Jamie was, of course, delighted to have Mum and Dad back together, and asked his dad how he was. Jamie carried on chatting, because this was the first time he had seen Harry in twelve months.

CHAPTER 33

NEW YEAR 1941

Harry took a couple of days to settle down. He was on his own for the most part of each day as the women were working on the farm, mucking out or milking. Harry got used to it quickly.

January was overcast, cold and wet. The ports around the south coast were now getting bombed again, but there was still the problem of shipping loss. Mary told Jamie that she had to sleep in an air raid shelter with others when she had last gone to London. She told him to thank the Lord that he had not been in London but here in the country.

There had been a few heavy showers of snow which made fieldwork difficult, therefore little could be done until the thaw came. The fields could not be worked. The next major event would be lambing time.

February arrived. The sheep were brought in to the lambing barns in preparation. Mr Wilson had Jamie check the perimeters to make sure there was no way foxes or any other predators could get in and take the newborn lambs. Jamie could see fox tracks in the snow, but the tracks showed that the foxes had been unsuccessful.

Everyone was now encouraged to eat raw carrots, as they were supposed to help you see in the dark. Jamie had been gnawing on carrots over the last couple of years but he didn't find his night vision any better. It did make a difference to his hunger though, as he was always hungry.

Right on time, the sheep started having their lambs, so quickly that in a matter of a few nights, it was all over. Mr Wilson said there was a good crop of lambs and that he was very pleased. The lambing had gone well, and now he was looking forward to sowing the fields, but the weather was still wet and windy. Farm work was almost at a standstill, but there was always some work to be done. Jamie found he wasn't involved in this work because it was school time for him, as now school was full time. Young Kenny, Alice's boy, was now Jamie's shadow. He followed Jamie wherever he went, and he was learning from Jamie. He wanted to go out in the early morning with Jamie when he went to clear his traps, but he wasn't allowed.

Jamie, Kenny and Kathleen were making their way to school. As they came to the farm, they met Mr Wilson, who thought all three were looking tired and hungry. They were looking very thin. Mr Wilson stopped them. He said, 'I want you, Jamie, to take this bag of potatoes back to your mum and tell her that I've opened the potato clamp and I'm giving all the villagers a few pounds of potatoes to help with their shortage of food. Can she come and help?' He told Jamie to get on his way to his mum. 'Kathleen, take Kenny on to school. Tell the teacher; tell her what I just told you. Potatoes will be free. No charge for the villagers. Go on to school.'

When Jamie got home and gave Mary and Harry Mr Wilson's message, they thought it was a godsend.

Mary worked hard that day until the clamp was nearly empty and returned late that afternoon to find that Harry had sat and peeled some potatoes for any of the ladies that came home first to cook something up for dinner. It didn't take long for hot potato soup to be made, then potato pancakes were underway.

The next day, in the afternoon, Mary and Alice went into town and got provisions for the whole family. There was little meat, but there was offal and some sausages (mainly made with bread). They were well laden and very tired when they got home.

The weather had finally begun to change. The rain showers were not as heavy, which meant work could start again. The ladies were earning again. In the evenings, Jamie returned to homework, and all three kids helped each other with their lessons. Jamie spent a great deal of time with his books, trying to catch up on his mathematics. Occasionally, wrapping up in heavy clothing, he went for a walk in the woods, trying to find anything edible that he could take home.

They were long days, but gradually the month came to an end. March started by washing the snow away. There was now light rain and mists every morning.

It was a long trudge to school, and seemed even longer every day because of the mud. Young Kenny found it heavy going. He wasn't as big as Jamie, and Jamie had to lend him a hand many times, just to get to school. Kathleen hated the mud as it mucked up her shoes. Jamie often heard her saying, 'I wish this was a London pavement.' They were all thin and hungry and had been for many days. Had it not been for the good gesture made by Mr Wilson, they probably would have become very ill through lack of food.

Now that the thaw had cleared the fields, the three of them didn't find getting to school so tiring.

CHAPTER 34

FOLLOW ORDERS

April was cloudy, wet and windy, but during the day there were glimpses of sunlight breaking through the clouds. The wind had the clouds scudding across the sky. Every so often, the clouds would break and sunbeams raced across the fields. Childlike Jamie, Kenny and Kathleen tried to run with the sunbeams but the sunbeams always won. They would all stop, out of breath. They were happy kids, and with a bit of laughter, carried on their way to school. It had been fun chasing the sunbeams!

By mid-April, the weather had improved and all the fields that had been ploughed last October were now ready for sowing. There was still one field that had never been ploughed by Mr Wilson. The field on the farm was where the hunters (horses) roamed freely. The horses had now been moved to a field on the other side of the farm and Jamie was no longer chased or bullied by them when he went to draw water from the well. It just had to be the gorse field right next to the forge. The horses had been there for years. It was also the best field on the farm for rabbiting. Jamie would sorely miss it and his catch of rabbits, which had always been a sustainable food supply in the spring, all the way through to the autumn. Now they would be gone.

Mr Wilson sent the two Land Army girls, Jean and Rita, and young Tom over with the tractor with chains to rip out all the gorse bushes. Tom was to take care of the burning of the gorse bushes and to ensure that the sparks from the fire were blowing away from the cornfields and the forge. With the first gorse bush ripped out, there were lots of rabbits; mostly young kits, which were not worth catching, but the big bucks and does were a different matter.

Mr Wilson had been ordered by the Ministry of Ag. & Fish to plant the field with cereal as there was a great demand.

Once the field had been cleared, the girls set to ploughing. When finished, they went away and left it, returning two weeks later when the field was quite dry. The girls brought, pulled behind the tractor, a slurry machine and proceeded to cover the field with the delightful smell of animal muck, which would linger for two or three days. Next, the girls brought the harrow in and raked the field, ready for the next stage of the procedure.

A couple of days later, they arrived with a seed drill and proceeded to work from one end of the field to the other until the whole field had been planted with wheat.

During all this work, Jamie had managed to catch sixteen rather large rabbits as they fled from their burrows in the hedges, either with snares or his rifle. Mary dealt with her share of the catch, cleaning them and getting them ready for the butcher in Chipping Norton, where she intended to barter for meat. The butcher would have the rabbits and Mary would perhaps come back with other cuts of meat, such as beef or even a bit of lamb; whatever she managed to persuade the butcher to exchange. Mary understood that this may not be legal, but she was prepared to take the risk. The butcher would either barter or just send her away.

The trip turned out to be successful and the butcher made an exchange. Mary also got some sausages and offal.

Once the field was completed, the rest of the month of April carried on, with all the general working on the farm being carried out.

Now they were getting ready for the Easter bank holiday. Jamie only now realised he had not even been to Sunday school, the way he used to at home, since he had been evacuated from London.

CHAPTER 35

FAMILY MATTERS

Springtime was rapidly approaching. It was on a Thursday that Jamie came home from school, bringing both Kenny and Kathleen safely with him, as usual, and they went straight into the kitchen for their tea. It was there that Jamie found Mary sitting at the table with an open letter on her lap. She had a lovely smile on her face. Mary told Jamie to sit down as she had some good news. Harry had spent the last few days in hospital because his right leg had collapsed, but after a full examination, it was confirmed that it was OK and Harry just needed some physiotherapy. He was brought home by Mr Wilson in the buggy and he had been offered work. Mr Wilson saw no reason for Harry not to stay at the forge and work from there, as the job was bookkeeping, and he could come to the farm once a month for Mrs Wilson to go over the books with him.

Harry thanked Mr Wilson for all that he was doing for the family. He'd found home a for them, given them work, looked after Jamie. He felt there was no way he could ever repay such a debt. Mr Wilson told him not to worry about things like that. He was only too pleased to have the help on the farm. There were no young men available as they were all in the forces, so help would continue to be needed all the time they were on the farm.

Mary said she was going to make a pot of tea and something to eat for them both as they hadn't eaten since first thing that morning. Alice sent Jamie to bring in the tea and sandwiches that she had recently made. Mary took over and started to tell Jamie, Alice and Kathy what it had been like in London on her last visit. She would tell Lillian, at dinner time, all that she had seen. She then told them how the hospital was shored up with sandbags against bomb blast. It had remained open throughout the raids as

74

there were many casualties throughout London. She said how there were bombed-out buildings, with rubble everywhere, but that people were still going out to work. On one occasion she saw a man going into his shop through his front window as the glass front of the shop had been blown out. She told them that Harry would have to exercise his right leg for a couple of months as it was weak from the muscle damage after being burnt. This would probably be over the rest of summer but now he had a job it would be much better than going for physiotherapy.

Jamie got up, went outside and sat on the wall to digest all he'd heard about his dad. He realised his dad was getting better but if he needed help, Jamie would be to there to do his best for his dad.

It was now two weeks before May and Jamie was on his way to school. He stopped off at the farm and asked Mr Wilson if, when his dad was better and able to walk, there would be any other work. Mr Wilson stopped Jamie short and said, 'Jamie, this is between us adults. When your dad is fit and thinks he can do a different job, I have no doubt I can find something for him to do. It is not up to you to ask, it is between your dad, mother and me. Now, go on off to school with you.'

Jamie bowed his head and started off for school. He was busy thinking. In just five years, he would have to leave school and start work. He wondered, what work? Would he still be in the country, working on a farm, or would the war have ended and he would be back in London?

CHAPTER 36

WEATHER PROBLEMS

May started cool but dry, with the threat of showers. There was still a week before the Easter bank holiday. The fields were all showing signs of fresh growth. The trees were late opening their buds. Jamie was thinking about the church parades. Would they still be able to carry on in London? He was remembering how he liked to see the houses with statues of the Madonna in their windows.

The news on the radio talked about how damage from the bombing on London, which was now infrequent, had given people the chance to tidy up some of the shopping areas and how life was again moving in London. Places like Liverpool and Birmingham, Manchester and other big towns were recovering after the end of the German onslaught. Jamie talked to Mary about this and she told him she didn't think they could live in London, as most of the houses where they lived, even St John's church nearby, had been on fire and crumbling when she had left to come to Jamie. Nearly everything there was burning and collapsing. 'Everything has changed in London, son,' she said. Then, 'Getting back to living here, Jamie, life is pretty good. You have missed those terrible sights. You have grown up very fast here, and I'm pleased about that. We better get back. There is still work for me to do and school for you.'

It was mainly wet but with dry spells. 'Not looking good for harvest, but we hope that the next few months will be dry. That would be helpful,' Mr Wilson told Jamie when they were talking, 'But it will help with potatoes.'

Jamie took Kenny to school each day but found school boring and preferred to work on the farm, but the weather was preventing this. Jamie was waiting for the summer to arrive when he would be needed as one of the 'kids in the corn', as Mr Churchill had described them.

Jamie had to go further afield to set snares as there were no rabbits near now. Mr Wilson told him to go to the far side of the farm where he kept the small herd of cows. That was a good half mile away. Jamie had to set out much earlier to clear these each morning and although Mary wanted whatever Jamie could bring in, she told Jamie it would have to stop, as he was still a young boy and things concerning his growing up must be considered. Jamie thought he was grown up and was very disappointed that his mum didn't think so, but he did as Mary told him. He set out a couple of snares in the hedgerows, but with little success.

Near the end of the month, the weather had at last changed and summer was on its way. There were warmer, drier days, which meant that Jamie could stay up later. Mary undertook some home teaching, reading, writing and arithmetic (known as 'the three Rs') however her own grammar wasn't very good.

Life went on as usual, with both work and education. Jamie had to be reminded that he would be 10 years old this year and his schooling would stop when he became 14. For any further education he would need to pass a scholarship exam. That wasn't likely, here in the village school. They must now considerer another school. Mary would give it some thought.

CHAPTER 37

CUT BACK ON STOCK

The weather was damp but with sunny days; not very different to April. It had to change soon. This was the prayer on the lips of farmers all over the country.

As usual, Jamie talked to Mr Wilson, as he looked upon him as a second father. Each day, Jamie took Kenny to school. That's when Jamie learnt most of the news. Mr Wilson told him he had to reduce his sheep flock as well as his dairy herd as more and more land was going to be put to the plough. Jamie asked if he was still able to get fresh milk each day as normal. The answer was, 'Yes, of course, if I can keep the small herd.' Mr Wilson was able to keep his two sows and one boar, but as soon as any piglets came and were big enough, they would be sent to market and probably become bacon. The trotters would almost certainly become glue and the skin would be turned into leather, to go towards the war effort. Jamie thought about that and said, 'Poor little things. Glad I'm not a pig.'

General work carried on on the farm and Mr Wilson and Jamie talked almost every day. The weather started to change. It was just a little bit warmer and drier, which was really what was wanted. So much work could now be done on the farm. An inspection of all the crops showed that they were good. Jamie was fretting at school. Although his writing was now fair, his grammar and spelling were terrible. All his words were spelt phonetically. He needed a lot of primary education in a bigger, London-style school. Mary would consider sending Jamie to stay with his grandmother in outer London to complete his education over the next four years.

A letter from Mary's father with the good news that Mary had wanted put a smile on her face.

The last few days were sunny and warm.

CHAPTER 38

A GOOD HARVEST

The May sunshine did not last and June came in cloudy and wet. The harvest, which had been looking good, now suffered. Mr Wilson, talking to Jamie, said, 'The outlook for harvest looks pretty bad for the summer but if we have good and fair weather for the next couple of months, we should save it late in August. Jamie, this life is full of setbacks: you never know what's going to happen and this is particularly true in farming. When you go back to living in London, you'll soon forget this time in your young life.' Jamie thought about this and said, 'I don't think so; life here on the farm with you, Mr Wilson, and Mrs Wilson has been just great, ever since I came to live with you. This I will always remember. I've had a wonderful time. It could never have been like this in London, and I would never ever have earned any money like the ten-shilling note you give me every month. I have been saving that money the way Mrs Wilson showed me when she bought me that money box last Christmas. I didn't buy presents this year, there wasn't much in the shops, and I have saved four pounds sixteen shillings and eightpence. I don't know what I could spend it on, but I'll keep it so that I have some money for when I do go back to London.' Mr Wilson said, 'It could be quite a while before you go back to London, Jamie, but you will one day. There is still a war on and Mr Churchill told us that there is a long way to go and we farmers must try and grow more food if possible. Your mum and Alice are still working and will decide when you leave, but we will always remember you. Now off to school with you.'

It was the 23rd and Jamie went to school with some questions about what he had heard on the radio the day before. He had to ask Mr Stevens. Late that morning, in the history/geography lesson (Mr Stevens taught both together) Jamie said, 'Where is

Russia and how big is it?' He had heard that Germany had decided to attack it. Jamie then asked, for the first time, the big question: 'Why is there a war at all?' Jamie had, after all, begun to wonder what it was all about. He said he had heard his mum say, 'The last war was supposed to be the war to end all wars', so why was there another one?

Mr Stevens tried to explain that Germany wanted to get bigger and had invaded Poland, a country next to Germany, and Great Britain had gone to the aid of Poland and declared war on Germany.

Jamie had a lot to think about. Who were the good and who were the bad people? Now Jamie had something to ponder.

That evening, he talked to Harry about what Mr Stevens had said and when Harry told him about Adolf Hitler being a dictator who had made even his own people afraid of him, Jamie thought that the Germans must be the bad and we must the good.

That night, Jamie slept well.

The next day was a bright and sunny day full of the promise of summer. Jamie decided it was far too good for school. He delivered Kenny, as usual, then turned around and walked down the lane leading to the brook. He went through the coppice and found a clear area right beside the brook, put down his bag, spread his jacket, then stretched out on the ground, looking up at the clear blue sky. The insects' buzzing was loud and along with the babbling of the brook, made Jamie relax. Being alone was calming for Jamie. He just lay there, enjoying the long grass and the morning; no work today. He ate his homemade cheese and tomato sandwich and said to himself, 'This cheese tastes mild, almost tasteless, and I spent hours shaking that leather bag until the milk stopped slopping and sounded more like a lump. Then mum had opened the bag, taken out the lump, which was some kind of cheese... well, it is edible.'

Now he lay back and soon he was sleeping.

There was a loud crash and Jamie jumped awake. He had thought it was the sound of a bomb in his dream, but no; it was a thunder clap. The sky was dark.

Jamie jumped up, grabbed his gear and ran until he got to the village school. He was drenched. That was the heaviest shower

Jamie had ever seen. The teacher was not happy and told Jamie to run home as fast as he could and get out of his wet clothes as soon as possible.

As he got near the cottage, he saw Mary and Alice standing by the front door. There was a big puddle just inside the gate and as he splashed through it, Mary and Alice turned and saw him: a wet, bedraggled boy. Mary grabbed Jamie and brought him in. She was stripping him as he came in. Alice came with a blanket and wrapped it around Jamie as he was shivering with the cold. Hot water was soon heated and Jamie was having a hot bath, then he was quickly put to bed.

Jamie was dreaming he was back among his friends, playing in the streets with their own style of football, a tennis ball. He was cold, then very hot. He was delirious. Mary was beside him, mopping him with cold water as he drifted in and out of sleep.

He woke with a start, nearly knocking a cup out of Mary's hand. She gently pushed him back under the covers and told Jamie to keep covered up. Through the window, Jamie saw the moon as he lay back and went to sleep.

Jamie woke up and could see the sunshine and hear the cockerel crowing in the farm. He wanted the gazunder and he was starving. He called for his mum but Harry came and he could see Jamie was better. He left for a short while and came back with a bowl of porridge with a little honey, which Jamie ate. He felt a bit better.

Harry sat with Jamie for a while and told him that he had been unwell for several days and it had upset Mary, but she had to go back to work.

The next day Jamie wanted to get up. He was wondering about his snares and he knew he should go to school but his mum said 'No!' so Jamie lay back.

Later, Mary told Jamie he had been in bed for four days with a fever and that was what came of playing truant from school. 'Don't do it again. You can get up later.'

Jamie thought, four days! He started getting up and found he felt quite weak. He would have to wait a few more days before he could go to school.

The weather for the rest of the month of June came in warm and dry, although often with fine clouds. This helped to ripen the cornfields.

Jamie had been unwell for a week but now the harvest was being done and Jamie was at last able to get out to help. He felt happier now as he had sat with Harry most of the time while he worked on invoices and deliveries. Now, outside, he was feeling good.

Harvest was still hot, dusty work, with the Land Army girls working the reapers. It was all the villagers and the kids doing the stooking, leaving them to dry out, ready for the threshing and the harvesting of the corn.

It was a better harvest than Mr Wilson had envisaged. Jamie was also very pleased. He had found a lot of wild fruits. Some were still not quite ripe, therefore the wildlife had not yet taken their share. Jamie's store in one of the sheds was now filling up nicely and Mary was already preserving fruit and veg, keeping them in the storeroom Mary had been saving with a view to taking it to London. Mary felt it was time the family was back together.

Mr Wilson paid off most of the workers now that the main harvest had been done.

Harry and Mary had now made up their minds about Jamie going to a bigger and better school for his last four years in education. At the dinner table, Mary announced that she, Harry, Jamie and Steven would be returning to London at the end of the month.

Jamie didn't know what to do, as he loved it there and could hardly remember London. What would it be like after all that bombing? Also, there were still bombing raids; few and far between, true, but still raids.

He said he didn't want to go. He wanted to stay there.

Harry was strict and rather rough as he turned and harshly said to Jamie, 'As a kid, remember your place. You'll do as you're told.'

Jamie went off to sit in the corner of the room in a sulk.

Alice and Lillian agreed it was time to go back to London, but they would stay for a little while longer, as it was a great life.

The heavy night bombing was now over apparently, but they were still reluctant to say when they would return to London, as there were still bombing raids. Mary said they would leave at the end of June as they both felt it was for the better. Mary felt Jamie must go to a bigger school for the last four years of his schooling as he would have to earn his living when he left school at 14.

The day they were all prepared was the last Friday of June. Mr Wilson had paid them and wished them good luck. He turned to Jamie and said, 'Jamie, lad, I will miss you the most. I feel you're like a son to me. Don't forget us and come back to see your other mum and dad someday.'

The old pram was loaded with all of Mary's cooking gear and a couple of boxes, mostly filled with food from the farm cold room. They said their goodbyes to Alice, Kenny, Kathy and Lillian, then with Harry helping Jamie push the pram and with Mary carrying Steven and two bags, they set off for Chipping Norton for the last time.

CHAPTER 39

GRANDFATHER'S PLACE

The journey into London was straightforward until they arrived at Paddington station and alighted. They had to find where Harry's friend, with his small van, was parked. Once found, they put the boxes into the van. Mary's cooking utensils were all placed inside, along with the food boxes. The old pram was dumped on a nearby bomb site as its springs were broken and it was of no further use. It had served its purpose well.

Jamie and Harry were in the back of the van with all the equipment, while Mary and Steven sat in the front with the driver. Jamie was quite bewildered by the sounds, and with the twists and turns that had to be taken from central London out to the suburbs near Eltham, to a place called Black Fen.

Their journey was bumpy as the road still had some rubble on it. When they reached Eltham, it was a lot cleaner. This was the first time Jamie had been in one of these new-fangled automobiles and he was not at all impressed. It had been a bumpy, uncomfortable ride and he had seen little out of the back window as they drove out of London. The burnt-out buildings and broken houses had made it impossible for him to recognise any of it. It all went past in a blur. Jamie was wondering, what did the part of London he'd known look like now?

Eventually the scenery changed and there were no more damaged buildings. The houses looked more normal, but still different to those Jamie remembered. They were smaller, shorter in height, and some were only single storey. They, he learned later, were called bungalows.

The van stopped. Mary got out, went around the back, opened the door and told Harry and Jamie it was OK to get out. They did so and Harry went with Mary, leaving Jamie to start unloading the van.

Jamie stood by a gate leading into the garden of a tall house. He looked towards the door of the two-storey house, with its good-sized garden. Leading from the gate there was a pathway and a man was walking towards him; he was a tall, elderly man dressed in grey trousers with a white shirt and a white cardigan. As he got closer, Jamie could see that he had white hair, a large white moustache and a kindly face. He was smiling at him. It wasn't someone he knew but he felt that he should. Mary came quickly up the path, caught up to the man and they arrived at the gate together. Mary said, 'Jamie, this is my father, your grandfather. You can get to know your grandfather.' Then she left Jamie alone with this new grandfather. It was his grandfather who broke the silence, saying, 'Hello, Jamie. It's been a very long time since we last met. In fact, over six years, because we lived so far apart. We were unable to travel as your grandmother is unable to walk. You will meet her later as your mum and dad, along with you children, will be staying with us for a while.'

Jamie looked at his grandfather and thanked him. As they moved into the house, Jamie paused and looked around as he followed his grandfather. Jamie looked around the hallway, which was small, with a staircase leading up to the next floor. On the left of the short passageway was a door into the front room and directly ahead was the door to a small kitchen (no black kitchen range here). It had a small oven, a table and chairs and an armchair facing the back door, looking out over a large garden. Jamie saw that it was well planted out. He could see that there were runner beans, potatoes sprouting, also tomato plants and carrots still growing. There was a lovely gooseberry bush and the gooseberries on it were beginning to ripen, turning golden. There were raspberry canes, laden with raspberries. Jamie thought, if Grandad doesn't pick all this fruit soon, the birds will take it! He had to tell his Grandad about that. His grandfather said, 'We'll do that tomorrow, Jamie. It seems your time in the country has taught you a great deal. We will be good friends because I love gardening.'

Upstairs were three bedrooms and a toilet. Jamie thought, this is much better than having to go out and use a hole in the ground, like they had to do back at the forge! Jamie was fascinated with the chain action and decided that later he would find out how it worked.

Mary had taken charge and had started preparing a dinner as they were hungry after all the traveling. She had stored most of her stuff out in the garden shed. Now, making sure that everything was under control, she was cooking dinner while Jamie explored the garden with his grandfather.

Both front and back gardens were inspected and lots of comments were passed by Jamie to his grandfather and his grandfather listened to what he thought was good. Jamie felt it was worthwhile. They were in the garden when a wailing sound started. Jamie realised it was a siren, warning them of a possible enemy bombing. Jamie turned to his grandfather and said, 'What do we do now, Grandad?' His grandfather replied, 'Nothing, we just have to stay here. Sit on the bench, wait and see what happens.'

Jamie and his grandfather just sat in the garden, looking up into the bright, blue sky. Jamie could see aircraft high up in the sky; black spots all wheeling around with some bigger aircraft flying in a straight line. Suddenly one of the big ones burst into flames, then another, with black smoke, started to come down. The smaller planes were much faster. They looked like birds fighting in the air. Jamie's grandfather said to him, 'Jamie, that is where men are shooting and killing each other. That's what war is all about. It's wrong but it's a necessary evil, and is not pleasant.'

After a short while, Jamie could see an aircraft burning and falling and there were a couple of parachutes in the air. Soon the sky was clear of aircraft as they seemed to disappear.

A little later, a wailing sounded again, but this was a single note which notified that the enemy action was over. It was all clear. Jamie and his grandfather went in and had some afternoon tea with Mary.

CHAPTER 40

ANOTHER NEW HOME

It was several days later when Mary told Jamie they would have to walk into Eltham and get registered as homeless; displaced people from London in need of a home somewhere, anywhere. It was needed soon. It took nearly all day to do this. Mary was told that she may have to apply to Bexley council as well.

Jamie's grandfather took him in to meet his grandmother in the bedroom. She was sitting up in a very large bed. She was, in fact, a very large lady herself; considerably overweight, due to ill health. She put her arms around Jamie, held him tightly and gave him a very long kiss on the forehead. When Jamie was free, he sat back and looked. He said to himself, she is a nice lady, round-faced with a nice smile and short, straight, grey hair. She held him again, giving him another big kiss. She said she loved seeing him after so long, how he had grown to be such a handsome young man and how sorry she was that she had been unable to see him before today.

His grandmother, just like himself, was full of questions. They sat and talked and this took up most of the morning. Jamie told his grandmother all about living in the country. All this took place while Mary had gone to register them and to see if there was a home for them in the very near future. From what Mary was told at the interview, it seemed unlikely that there would be a home quickly but as she had two children, she would be housed as soon as possible.

Mary's request for housing was successful after several weeks. She was allocated a requisitioned house. The owners had gone to Canada at the outbreak of war and the house stood empty. It must have been an extremely lucky house, because it was only half a house; the other half was a bomb crater. The house that they were to live in had no neighbours on one side.

The house was situated just outside Black Fen, in between Black Fen and Welling. The nearest shops were in a place called The Green. The streets were all named after the counties of Kent. Here they would be able to settle down to a normal life. Mary would register Jamie at a school called Westwood Secondary Modern for Boys, near to a place called Falkenwood. Jamie decided to investigate the area as soon as possible.

Shortly after the first week of settling in, Jamie was taken to see the big school for the first time. A siren sounded and Mary and Jamie made their way to a shelter. The sound of gunfire was heard, also the sound of bombs exploding, but they were far away, in central London.

Listening to the radio that evening, it was announced that Rudolf Hess had been arrested upon his landing in Scotland. He was the deputy to Hitler. No further news was given.

CHAPTER 41

WESTWOOD SECONDARY SCHOOL

Mary made sure Jamie was dressed in a clean blue shirt, short grey trousers (new, of course), black socks, a black jacket trimmed with green and black shoes. Jamie felt uncomfortable as he had to wear these clothes especially for school. They were the school uniform, except not everyone could get them, due to shortage of the material.

They arrived at the school. Jamie was ushered into a place which seemed like going to church on a Sunday, something he hadn't done for such a long time. The school, to Jamie, looked big and rather frightening. They made their way to the imposing entrance. A person told them to sit and wait; the headmaster would see them as soon as he was free.

Later, Mary was ushered into the headmaster's office. Jamie sat and waited.

After a short while, Mary came out with the large man. The man came and told Jamie that he was going to take him to a class. Jamie looked up at this giant, then stood up and followed him. Not another word was spoken until they reached a room, full of other children about Jamie's age. Mary was now free to go, and she returned home.

Jamie had studied the man. He was very tall and heavy. He also noticed an unusual thing: that his right hand had no index finger or thumb. It looked as though they had been removed. This was something that Jamie would always remember: the sight of a man without a thumb, holding a cane as they walked. He was to learn that the man could use that hand just as well as the other.

He had been taken to a classroom with about eleven boys sitting at individual desks, not like the benches at the school in Dunthrope. Jamie was shown to a desk and told to sit down and not talk. Jamie did as he was told and tried to understand what the teacher was talking about, but he was completely lost. What was written on the blackboard was completely alien to anything he had ever seen. It was all numbers and signs.

In the next class, there was a book to read and study but it was in no English that he knew, with words like 'vowel' or 'consonant'. Jamie was, again, lost. Who was this William Shakespeare, anyway?

When the siren sounded, the class were told to make their way to the big assembly hall. When the all clear was given, they returned to the class. Jamie just sat, and the lesson went over his head.

In only one class did he shine. He came awake as the teacher was talking about farmers and how they had been told by the government to work harder, giving the impression that it was easy work. Jamie's hackles were rising and he called out in anger, 'You're wrong! It's very hard work! They get up at dawn and work until dark.' The teacher told Jamie to be quiet and said that he would speak to him later. The rest of the class gave Jamie some very hard stares.

Jamie sat quietly for the rest of the day. He didn't speak a word to anyone; even when the teacher spoke to him, Jamie went dumb.

The school day ended.

On the way home, two boys called Jamie a dummy and told him he should be in the lower classes with the other dimwits.

Sitting down to dinner that evening, Mary asked Jamie about school. Jamie went dumb and would not respond. Mary knew something was wrong, and after many questions from Mary, Jamie finally repeated the words of the two schoolboys about him being a dimwit. Mary just looked at Jamie, said nothing and finished dinner in a quiet mood.

CHAPTER 42

A SHOW OF ANGER

That evening, after Jamie had gone to bed, Mary and Harry were talking. Mary decided that she would go to the school with Jamie the next day. She was going to have a flaming row with the headmaster, Mr Andrews. She was extremely angry and needed to speak to someone to relieve her anger.

As she had said, next morning, she and Jamie went to school together and instead of allowing Jamie to go straight to his class, Mary took him to the headmaster's office and told him to sit outside and wait, then demanded to see the headmaster, which she did, eventually.

At her interview with Mr Andrews, she informed him that Jamie had had the most education available while he had been evacuated and had been expected to work on a farm, as most of the children had. He had not been attending the village school for more than a few hours per day and that was the reason for his education being basic, to say the least. However, with some help from herself and her friends, and also with Jamie's intention to learn, he had managed to teach himself how to write. 'Badly, I know,' she added. Mary said she was aware that Jamie's grammar and spelling were bad, very bad, but that's why she had brought him here, because he had barely four years to go before he would be forced to leave school.

The headmaster listened intently and eventually agreed that he had put Jamie into a class according to his age and that Jamie's education had obviously suffered badly due to the war. He was prepared, now, to advance Jamie by putting him in a class given more individual attention, for those in the same situation as Jamie. There he could continue with his education, bringing him up to the standard he should be at, at his age.

Mary was satisfied with this and agreed that it was probably the best way forward for Jamie, however she was intensely angry that other boys had referred to her son as a dimwit and demanded an apology for this and said that the school should be informed the people are not dim witted, but educationally starved due to the war years and evacuation. Mr Andrews agreed that at the assembly tomorrow, he would say this to all the school members and inform the teachers that no such remarks should be made again to any of the pupils in the school.

Jamie was taken to another class with boys like him, who had suffered badly with their education during the first two years of war. Jamie settled in the for the rest of the day. Mary went home not quite so angry and at least felt that the headmaster, Mr Andrews, had listened and done something about it.

Every day, the sirens sounded and interrupted the lessons. They were more of nuisance as they were not local.

Harry had found a light job and was now living at home. As a family, they were making decisions about the children. They discussed Jamie's future and agreed that they would give him evening classes all the time they were able. Steven would stay at home with Mary as school for under-fives was not available. When Jamie came home every afternoon he would sit and read to Mary the notes he had made or talked about the lessons he had had. Mary felt she was also learning and, in the evening, after his watch, Harry, too, would help Jamie with his homework. Harry helped Jamie start painting again, as a pastime and for relaxation.

On his way to work, Harry was looking into a second-hand bookshop, of which there were many, those days; stuff from bombed-out houses. He found an almost complete set of the Encyclopaedia Britannica. He bought them quite cheaply, for just two pounds, and thought these would help Jamie with his education.

Jamie started to read book one slowly. He became an avid reader. Most of the subjects he liked and thought he would like to learn a great deal more about. He became a young boy that would read almost anything put in front of him: paperbacks, hardcover books, newspapers and comics; he read them all from cover to cover, especially one comic in particular, called *The Champion*. It was all words, not pictures.

Over the next few months, Jamie did nothing more than read and absorb knowledge. This was his prime target, of course, but caused some problems for Jamie as he never really made any friends with whom he could play or talk. Jamie spent a great deal of time alone or reading books. This was to become the normal way his day was spent. Very often there was an air raid warning and the siren sounded. Nothing happened close.

Jamie never made any close friends. Somehow, other boys had little interest in the same things as Jamie.

He was now a very different lad and it wouldn't be long before his 10th birthday.

CHAPTER 43

A FRIEND

Jamie continued to work very hard as he wanted to move up in the school ranking: 'C' to 'B' then to 'A', the higher classes. He had given Mary whatever money was left in his money box, as things were tight in the house. Dad's wages were the main income. There was no hunting anymore. All the food that they had brought with them was now gone. Mary was struggling to keep the family fed.

Jamie still had no close friends. He was a loner. None of the other boys had the same interests as Jamie. He became more and more involved in his art classes, at which he was showing reasonable talent. A lot of the other boys called Jamie a big head as he simply knew a great deal more about life than they did, due to his experiences on a farm.

Mary now decided to help Jamie with arithmetic. She wasn't very good at it herself, except when she went shopping and used money. She now took Jamie under her wing. Every time she carried out any expenditure, she sat down with Jamie and went through each item. She then taught Jamie how to add and subtract each of the items from the bill. This taught Jamie quite a bit of arithmetic but it was only addition and subtraction. At school, the other parts of arithmetic came with multiplication and division and learning to do this in his head without paper and pencil. With the times tables he had learnt in the village school, he was making good headway; then came long division sums. This took Jamie a little longer to master.

Jamie was an avid learner; it wasn't long before he had mastered most sums set by the teachers in the school. His education was taking leaps and bounds forward. His knowledge was expanding rapidly.

He was 10 years old on the 15th of September. This day was nominated by Mr Churchill as Battle of Britain day. Now some changes would take place because Jamie would have to sit school exams to show that he had learnt enough to be considered for advancement into a new class level.

Jamie had now seen his 10th birthday and sat the educational test. He had passed, with a low mark, but it was sufficient. He was now moved from the C, the lowest stream, into the B stream. It would be a few years before he could get into the A stream.

It was some time later he found that the reason he couldn't make friends easily was because he did not play football or cricket. He wasn't interested in rugby. In fact, he had no real aptitude for games at all. As nearly every boy in the school played some type of ball game, he was always left on his own. His interests were of a more academic nature: painting and reading any book he could lay his hands upon. He thought he would like to play board games, although he knew of no one that could teach him, nor anybody that played.

Jamie loved nature books, knowing what he did about living on the farm. He showed an interest in insect life. He liked most insects but he had a strong dislike of wasps.

September was an eventful month for Jamie as he at last found a friend. It was in the playground one morning at break. He saw a young lad sitting in the corner of the playground reading a book. Jamie's curiosity aroused, he walked over and asked the lad what his book was about. Was it interesting? 'What is your name?' Jamie had come straight to the point. The young lad said that his name was Roy, then he told Jamie the book was about a game called chess. Jamie became intrigued about this, as Roy tried to explain the game to him. He told Jamie that he would need a chess board and chess pieces, then he could explain what the pieces could do and what they were called when they had a set. Then he'd show Jamie how the pieces worked. Jamie was really looking forward to getting a chess set and learning how to play.

That evening, at dinner with his parents, Jamie told them about meeting Roy and what they had talked about, and said that he would like to learn how to play chess. After talking together,

Mary and Harry agreed that it was a good idea and that they would try and help.

On his way to work, Harry looked in a second-hand shop, to see if here was anything that would be helpful. Lo and behold, there was a chess board and a wooden chess set. It was marked up at ten pence; not expensive, as it was a second-hand set. Harry purchased it.

That evening he gave it to Jamie and told him it was his delayed birthday present. Jamie could now talk to his friend Roy and see if he would teach him how to play chess. Jamie was pleased as punch. Now he would be able to learn a game and at last he had somebody he thought would be his friend.

Lessons from now on were going to be a lot harder but Jamie was looking forward to it. He would learn a great deal more and hopefully a great deal faster.

Jamie's friend Roy had, over several weeks, taught Jamie how to play chess. This had hardened their friendship as they met and talked a great deal.

The war seemed to have faded away after the last terrible raid on Southampton. The RAF now controlled the skies over the United Kingdom. The population seemed to have settled down to a quieter life, for a short period of time, not forgetting the men in the forces.

The military traffic had increased quite a lot. Every so often the siren would sound as there were some night time aircraft flying during the night but little bombing. It was announced on the radio that German troops had attacked Russia and were moving fast towards Moscow. The newspapers and the radio were full of it. Jamie asked Harry if it would make much difference as now Hitler was fighting Russia as well as England. Harry told Jamie it could make a big difference and make things a lot easier for England as Germany was now fighting on two fronts; and any army officer would tell you: it's a mistake, a very big mistake, to split your army to fight two different wars at the same time. Jamie exclaimed, 'Good! I'm glad he's made a mistake. I hope he suffers for it!'

At school, Jamie asked a great deal of questions in history lessons. He wanted to know how big Russia was, also how far from England it was. He also wanted to know if it was only during wartime that the people of the cities of Great Britain could volunteer for something called the home front. Also, could children like himself join? The teacher told the class that they were too young to volunteer but what they were doing, collecting paper and scrap metal, was volunteer work. It had been introduced during the First World War, 1914-1918, and was being resurrected for this war. They were also told that, for now, men and women had to register to be called into service. It was called conscription and it had restarted that year, 1941.

New posters started to appear on walls and lampposts. One was 'Dig for Victory', also 'Get rid of lawns, turn them into vegetable plots.' Jamie and Mary knew just how to do that. It wasn't long before the front lawn was ready to become a vegetable plot that would be planted with potatoes, peas, runner beans and carrots, all in high expectation of a good crop next year. The back garden would also been planted out with not only vegetables but raspberry canes and other fruit bushes.

Mary now had a rabbit in a hutch at the bottom of the garden with an outside run. The rabbit was destined to be their Christmas dinner. They were quite used to eating rabbit and quite enjoyed it, so knew that when it was Christmas and it was big enough, it would be on the table. Mary wanted to keep some chickens, however trying to find wire to make a coop was out of the question; it was just not available. Jamie went looking around the alleys. He found a small roll of rusty wire and took it home. Harry said it might work. He would see what he could do for Mary, in making a coop.

It wasn't long before it became obvious that there wasn't enough wire, so no chickens.

The rest of October was relatively quiet, and Jamie carried on with his education. He spent morning break with Roy, playing chess. It was keeping Jamie well occupied. Now he began to look forward to Christmas, which was still two months away. He would have to start trying to find something for his mum and dad and, of course, Steven, who was now growing up quite fast and was a chubby little boy. Jamie was very proud of him.

CHAPTER 44

AUTUMN 1941

The month of November came in cold, wet and cloudy, just as it had been during October. It was now that Jamie decided he would like to have a bicycle, but bicycles weren't being made for sale because of the war. He decided to try and scavenge for the parts of a cycle from the alleyways and bomb sites. At the back garden of all the houses there were alleyways. These alleyways became rubbish dumps. Jamie decided to start there, but after two weeks of looking, he found nothing. Harry said maybe he could buy a new bike after the war. Jamie just had to accept there would be no bicycle for now.

So far, autumn had been normal, but it was nearing the end of the year and would soon change. Jamie was hoping the house they were now living in would be warmer than the old forge had been. The truth was, Jamie felt quite upset; no bicycle and no hope of one.

As usual, Jamie marvelled at the changing of the year, the colours in the trees red, orange and yellow. The colours of the leaves reminded him of the countryside. Next, they would all shed their leaves and prepare for the winter months. Still, plant life was challenging in the gardens. Not much could be done because soon the weather would be cold on the ground and later it would be frozen, with no chance of life coming through.

Life went on and the war also carried on. Jamie sat his end of term school education test and passed. He was very pleased, and so were Mary and Harry.

Through the month of November, food was getting very scarce. Jamie learned that the primary cause of this was that only a few ships in the convoys were getting safely across the Atlantic. They would just have to suffer. It was the German submarines that were taking a terrible toll on the merchant navy. The population of the UK would be kept hungry, slim and angry. They would also have to get used to starvation. Being British, they would not give in. They would suffer it without much complaint.

CHAPTER 45

MAKE DO AND MEND

December came in very cold and very wet and the rain was continuous. There was now nothing funny about standing in queues waiting to find out what was on sale. The only queue you stood in without complaint was for fuel. Coal was scarce and rations were scarce. People were given no more than one quarter of a hundredweight of coal.

Jamie and his mother stood in the queue, but not together. Mary gave Jamie the money to get his quarter of a hundredweight then she would get another quarter of a hundredweight. They would make their way home but not together, until well out of sight of the coal yard.

There were no overweight people in London in those days. Very many people were feeling extremely cold and uncomfortable. Lots of the elderly people suffered greatly with heavy heads and chest colds, often followed by pneumonia. A great many patients. Others just passed away at home during the winter months. More died than usual, was the radio report.

Jamie himself was now quite thin. At school they helped as much as they could. School dinners were not yet established, but teachers usually tried to find something at midday. There was never very much; often hot, watery soup and dry bread was all that they could manage, but it was a great help.

Jamie had learnt, when in the country, how to scrounge. He did just that, scrounging through the alleyways, where he could find extra fuel for the fire to keep the house warm, because it was essential not to get cold or catch a cold.

The war news was that on the 7th December, Japan attacked the United States of America in Pearl Harbour, sinking much of the American heavy battleships. This made America declare war on Japan and brought the USA into the World War.

Germany's campaign against Russia had come to a halt in a place called Stalingrad where the German army laid siege to that city. The radio broadcast was full of what had happened, however it was always sometime after the event. Jamie supposed this was so as not to tell too much to the enemy. But it was news, as far as England was concerned. England looked forward to the Americans becoming their Allies. The Americans, naturally, had declared war on Japan and Germany. Soon battles would commence. So far, the news had been good. The radio was full of the USA joining the fight, even the newspapers were full of it, what newspapers there were. Changes would take place from here on in. Now, of course, was the time to look forward to Christmas, not that there were very many things available to give as presents. The shops were mostly empty, although people were looking around for small things; anything that could be considered a Christmas gift. Harry was making wooden toys, primarily for Steven and some other children in the street. They went down well. Most neighbours bought something. He made toy forts for the boys and wooden puzzles. He also created a wooden man with a balancing rod in his hands, standing on a wooden tower. When the man was placed on the tower he balanced or even danced if you moved the rod slightly. It was ingenious, really. Harry was quite clever in his own way.

Of course, the poor old rabbit at the end of the garden had been fattened up well and truly. There was still some veg in Mary's store at the end of the garden, where it was kept cold. The garden, which had been dug up, and the front garden, were looking very bare. Planting had to wait until spring.

Christmas dinner was a quiet affair that year. There were no crackers and the only chains were the newspaper chains made by Mary and Jamie from old newspapers, flour and water paste. It was a very austere Christmas indeed. Mary, Harry and Jamie played and made it a nice Christmas for Steven. Mary had made Steven a kind of jumpsuit, which he was happy with. He was getting quite big! Jamie knew that Mary was sharing what little she had with him and Steven. He could get into mischief quicker than anyone Jamie knew. He clearly had a voice. if he wanted something, he let you know.

For Jamie, Mary had made a jumper from wool she had recovered from worn-out woollens and reknitted, striped with many colours. Jamie was pleased, as his only other jumper was falling apart.

After that 1941 December, life carried on. Everyone started going back to work and the grindstone of living began all over again. Queuing for winter fuel was a priority and, of course, food whenever it was available in shops. Everything was scarce. Christmas 1941 was a sad affair.

CHAPTER 46

BAD WARTIME NEWS 1942

January 1942 dawned and the weather came in as usual: cold, wet and overcast. A typical January morning. Jamie always had a strange feeling on the first day of the year which he never could explain. It was something to do with the winter daylight, cold, chilling, that made Jamie shiver, even though he wore his warm clothing.

Now, in the second week of the year, the news on the radio was full of what had happened in the Far East on 8th December. The British army held the Japanese off for twelve days before surrendering to an overwhelming Japanese force which now had control of Singapore.

At school, Jamie, again, was asking lots of questions about China, Singapore and the area of the Far East. Here, again, he was full of curiosity and learning more and more about geography. He was shocked to learn that it was the first time Britain had surrendered a colony to an enemy. The news was of the fall of Singapore and a later report that the Japanese had slaughtered all the wounded soldiers and all medical staff on Christmas Day.

Jamie, on his way home from school that evening, stopped and bought a late paper. He hurried home for tea. He sat and read the paper, knowing Harry would want to do the same when he came home from work. Jamie read that Mr Churchill had won a vote of no confidence. Jamie wondered, what did that mean? He'd ask Harry after tea. After teatime, Harry explained that Mr Churchill had been challenged by the government about the way he was handling the war and he had won that challenge. He was now considered the best politician for war in England.

Jamie spent the rest of the month either studying or queuing for food and fuel. It was a cold wet and windy month. During this time Mary had recycled some wool from other old woollens and knitted balaclavas for both Harry and Jamie and woolly clothes for Steven. Harry had a bit of a relapse and had to go off sick from work. He was off for almost three weeks. Money was now very short. Jamie and Mary both made sacrifices for Harry and young Steven. To keep warm at night, the beds had overcoats; threadbare, but they kept the beds a bit warmer.

Jamie, one morning after scraping the ice off the inside of the window, sat on the bed and thought: I'd finished doing this after we had left the forge, but at least the toilet is inside. Just so long as the pipes don't freeze up, everything will be OK.

January didn't change very much. Still cold and wetter than usual. Jamie still had to go out every day, either to school or, at weekends, shopping with Mary, queueing for this and that; whatever was on sale, wherever it was, trying desperately hard to find enough food to feed them through January. Harry was still off work, going into the third week of January. He felt that he was better and would soon go back.

Things were desperately hard. There was very little food. Mary had no money without Harry's wage coming in. She was finding it hard just to pay the rent, knowing something would have to be paid by the end of the month. Jamie heard Mary, in the kitchen peeling potatoes, say out loud to herself, not knowing Jamie was standing in the doorway, 'Please, God, don't let there be any illnesses with the children or me. Without me, I'm sure we would all perish.'

Jamie was shaken by this. He knew things were bad but hadn't thought about anybody getting sick.

Jamie stood, shocked, and wondered what would happen without his mum.

Still, the war went on. More bad news was coming from the Far East, also from the Sahara Desert, with the news that Germany had invaded North Africa.

CHAPTER 47

HARD TIMES AGAIN

Although it was still very cold, it was the rain that was the most troublesome. Every day, walking to school, Jamie swore to himself that one day, he would get a motor car, just to stay dry. It was inevitable that, when reaching school, he would be soaking wet. The heavy clothing he had had on the farm, and his wellies, had worn out or he had grown out of them. He missed them sorely. There were no buses going in the school's direction those days or anywhere nearby and so it had to be, as the saying, goes, 'by Shanks's pony.' It wasn't long before Jamie, like most of the class, had a head cold or a chesty cough. The very thing that Mary had dreaded. There were colds in the family, which meant that some sort of medication had to be bought. Cough mixture and Aspirin were the only remedies that were affordable. Galloways cough mixture was the main one and Jamie rather liked it but Mary had a recipe of her own. She chopped up the one remaining onion in the larder and what little sugar she could spare was put over the onion and left. The juice of the onion could be drunk as a cough mixture. It wasn't bad and also it worked.

Of course, now Jamie, Harry, Mary and Steven were hungry all the time. Life was grim, Jamie thought. Occasional air raid sirens sounded but nothing happened locally.

One Saturday, word was spreading that the coalman had a delivery in. What little money Mary had would have to go on coal. Both Mary and Jamie joined the long queue. Cold and wet, they each finally got their quarter of a hundredweight and managed to get it home. The garden was now empty, with nothing growing in it at all; the rabbit hutch was empty and likely to end up on the fire. The only green vegetables around were cabbages. There were also some turnips on sale and potatoes were also

available. Mary was able to make cabbage soups and other vegetable soups, which were filling but not so interesting, usually with
old bread, which was usually dry, like biscuits. It was the best that
could be done.

Mary asked Jamie to stay at home as she had to go out. She
didn't want to take Steven with her. Jamie stayed with Steven until
Mary returned home. It was some time later that Jamie noticed
Mary's rings were missing. Also her fur cape had gone. Jamie
knew Mary had found 'the corner shop' again; here we are again,
right back to where we started at the beginning of the war, using a
pawn shop. Jamie knew things were really bad and would only get
better when Mary had some money coming into the house.

One Sunday, the rain had stopped and dinner was over; what
little there was of it. All the shops were shut, as usual. The afternoon was going to be long and boring. Jamie, Harry, Steven and
Mary were sitting around the little fire when there was a knock on
the door. Jamie went, and upon opening the door, saw Grandad
standing there. Jamie stepped back and let him in. It was then that
Jamie saw the two bags he had. Jamie took one bag, Grandad
carried the other.

CHAPTER 48

GRANDAD, A GODSEND

Grandad went straight into the living room. Jamie followed with the bag. Grandad sat and asked Mary how she and the family were, commenting on how thin were looking. Giving the bag to Mary, he said, 'This may help a little.'

Mary had not been expecting her father and asked about Jamie's grandma. 'Is there a problem?' There wasn't, she was told. Jamie's grandfather told Mary that he couldn't stay as he needed to get home before dark. After a short while, he left.

When they were alone, Mary and Harry opened the bags and began to unload them. There was a small amount of meat, potatoes and a cauliflower. There was also bread and several other bits and pieces that the family could use. Both Mary and Harry were protesting, saying Grandad could not afford to give them this as he needed it for himself and Grandma.

Mary and Harry slowly continued emptying the bags. Lying in the bottom of one bag was an envelope. Harry opened the envelope slowly, wondering just what was inside. It was a five-pound note. Mary burst into tears, crying on Harry's shoulder. That money would keep the whole family for a month. Harry vowed that he would repay the money as soon as he could.

On Monday morning, Mary told Jamie, 'No school today, you're with me.' She had decided it was time to go shopping and spend some of the five pounds. Mary said, 'Thank you, God.' Jamie was to be her donkey.

First, they went to the butchers, as Mary had not been able to buy any meat for some time. Her rations coupons got more than she needed. She spoke to the butcher and before she could purchase anything, she produced the five-pound note and had to sign it in front of the butcher before she could spend any of it.

She bought various pieces of meat that would go a long way, but the best buy was a whole oxtail. The oxtail, which was off the rations, was going to make a few stews that would fill the family.

Mary did the rest of the family shop, finding a small amount of pearl barley which would bulk out the soups and casseroles, and purchasing any available vegetables, or anything else edible that they didn't have to queue for or that needed coupons. Jamie was loaded, and they made their way back home. They would live moderately well for the rest of the month and probably most of next month as well.

CHAPTER 49

HARRY'S NEW JOB

The month of February came in dry but turned to rain and snow. It now became very cold. The temperature dropped at the end of the first week and was freezing. This caused the small stock of coal and wood to be consumed very quickly. There was little or no action on the home front during that month. Jamie felt that school would now take priority for him. It would be a bit warmer. However, on his way home, he continued his search for fuel as an absolute necessity.

Harry and all the family's health improved, with the food building them up. Harry was fit enough to return to work and set out to secure a job. Within a week, Harry had found an office job in an engineering firm. The company needed engineers for the war effort and Harry was in the design office, using his skills there.

In March, there were fewer air raids. School took on a new outlook. It became strict about attendance, which made it difficult for Jamie to help at home. Jamie had to study hard, as he was to sit exams in three months; the midterm exams.

March 1942 was the first month that the radio news had very little to say about the war or what was happening abroad.

Jamie spent most of his free time, between errands and studying, reading books. He had been thinking about his friend Roy, whom he hadn't seen for a long time. He wondered how he was. He went to his room and sat down to write a letter to Roy. It was a friendly letter, telling Roy how he was feeling and that he was keeping well, also what he had been reading in his studies. He told Roy he was missing their chess games, plus a lot of trivia about school and the hardships at home. Finally, Jamie signed it, sealed it in an envelope, then realised he didn't have a stamp. He went to Mary and asked if she had such a thing. As usual, Mary had postage stamps in her purse. She nearly always had one. Jamie put the stamp on the envelope and took it outside. He put it in the letterbox, hoping that he would receive a letter back from Roy.

It was several weeks before Jamie got a reply. He wasn't to know that, for some time, Roy and his family had been living in Canada. This was to be their only communication for the rest of the war.

CHAPTER 50

DIGGING FOR VICTORY

As usual, April opened with sunshine and showers. Now Jamie could start on the garden, at long last. Mary told Jamie, so he didn't make any arrangements or plans for that weekend, that it would be spent working in the garden. On Friday, Jamie knew he would be working until dark on Saturday. There was a lot to do in the garden and trenches had to be dug for potatoes. He hoped Mary had managed to get some seed potatoes. Where there was an empty space, it needed to be dug over and prepared for other vegetables. What had been planted was showing through. Jamie hoped Mary had found other seeds as, without the seeds, the garden would be nothing.

That weekend, Jamie managed to prepare the long back garden for more planting, but he was absolutely exhausted by the end of the day and knew it would happen all over again the next weekend. Jamie just hoped it wouldn't rain, because that would make the ground very heavy for the next weekend, when he would be working in the front garden.

After dinner that evening, on the radio, it wasn't very good news for the UK. Most of it was about the Far East in Singapore. The Japanese had taken over from the UK army, rounded up all Europeans and taken them away to camps. Then, as usual, after the news, the traitor known as Lord Haw-Haw would boast about how Germany was winning the war; even though there was other news coming through that on the Russian front, Hitler's army had been brought to a halt. Reasons were not given but it was good news there. Then came further news about Japan. This time, they had attacked the island of Ceylon (Sri Lanka today) in two places. At the same time, they were attacking English domains.

After the news ended, Jamie asked Harry about the place called Ceylon and how important it was. The Japanese had attacked it twice, so it must've been important. Harry explained that Ceylon was at the base of India and that if Japan could conquer Ceylon, it could then attack India, which was very important to the British Empire. Jamie was getting rather confused about all this, because he had not learnt very much about the Empire or India, or even the island of Ceylon. It seemed like the Japanese Empire was conquering all the islands from China down to the Philippines and now attacking Ceylon. It seemed to Jamie that England was being pushed back, wherever it was.

A rather savage air raid attack on Exeter, in the West Country, was reported overnight. Mr Churchill made a statement, saying he thought it was a revenge attack because the UK had bombed the town of Lübeck in Germany. About that time, in London, the new Archbishop of Canterbury was enthroned. Jamie said to Harry, 'I wonder if God is on our side. I hope the new Archbishop asks him for some help.' Harry told Jamie that he probably did, every Sunday in church, 'Where, by the way, Jamie, you haven't been for a number of weeks. Not good enough you know, son.'

On the news that evening, it was reported that a new corp had been set up. Women only were being recruited into this new corp and it was to be called Women's Timber Corp. Their job would be to find suitable timber in woodlands for props in mines and other purposes, like making huts for the army and prisoner of war camps. Jamie thought, it just shows what war does: now it's the women who have to do the work, as there are very few grown men available.

April ran smoothly. With the sunshine and showers, gardening work could be going on and Jamie had managed to get the seeds planted in the front and back gardens with help, of course, from Mary and a little help from Harry. Steven also managed to scrabble about in the dirt, much to Mary's consternation. Clothes cost money and coupons. But Steven wanted to help in the garden and he was a determined little boy. He was learning the hard way.

CHAPTER 51

TROUBLE AT SCHOOL

Jamie listened to the news on the radio most evenings, along with his parents. Harry loved to listen to a comedy show call *ITMA* (*It's That Man Again*). It was Tommy Hanley's radio show and full of laughs.

The money Grandad had given Mary was almost gone, but now Harry was working, things began to improve. Soon they would be back on an even keel.

Jamie was getting taller but was still very thin and needing new clothes. Jamie was supposed to have a black and green school cap and tie, but for now he had only a second-hand tie. Jamie didn't care and when challenged at school by a teacher, he cheeked the teacher by saying, 'You want me to have a cap, then you buy it.'

For that, of course, he was sent to see the headmaster, presumably for punishment. Jamie, however, was not given the cane. A letter was sent to Harry instead.

Harry, naturally, told Jamie off for being cheeky and said that it shows the family up. 'Answering back to a teacher just isn't done and you will apologise and show more respect.' Jamie, of course, the next day, did say he was sorry to the teacher, even though he didn't really mean it.

It was now several weeks into May and a lot of news was coming in about the far east and a battle of the Coral Sea between America and the Japanese fleets. The German submarines were now penetrating close to the American shoreline. Some even got into the St Lawrence River, were detected, then chased out. That was only after sinking an English freight ship. Jamie thought, England doesn't seem to be doing very well. Now they were also defending the island of Malta. This was all bad news as far as

Jamie was concerned. The English were concerned about keeping Malta, as it was the gateway to North Africa. That was what the newsreader said on the news.

Now Jamie had lots of questions about where all these places were and why England were losing all these battles. Harry explained that it seemed to be the way war goes, but hopefully it would change and go the other way soon and the UK would have some good news.

Jamie turned his attention to the gardens. The seedlings were now beginning to show and weeding had to be done, as well as keeping birds off the young shoots. Mary had found and bought another rabbit, which was in the old, cleaned-up hutch which had almost gone on the fire. Steven was helping Mary feed it and clean its cage, as well as make sure the fenced run was OK. Even at his tender age, he had to learn the facts of life, one way or another. It wasn't very long before the family saw that Steven much preferred to play with the rabbit, even taking it out of its cage and sitting in the run just to cuddle it. Mary, of course, had to help him. He would have to learn over the coming months that this animal, which was so cuddly, was in fact destined to become Christmas dinner.

During the day, while working in the garden, Jamie thought of Mr and Mrs Wilson and wished he could be back on the farm, not having to stick to the daily routine of school.

In class, one day, Jamie was told by the teacher that he should not be working on the garden most evenings and weekends but should be doing homework. But they had to grow a lot of their own food as everything was in short supply.

That evening, Jamie sat down to write a letter to Mr and Mrs Wilson. He started by saying how much he missed life on the farm. He continued by telling them everything that had happened after leaving: the terrible sights he had seen in London, how he had found a grandfather and grandmother, how much Steven was growing and how he liked to sit in the garden and cuddle the rabbit, which was destined to be Christmas dinner. He told them how, at school, he never seemed to be good enough at exams. He had managed to pass, but only just. How he studied every day and was determined to get into the upper levels at school. He hoped they were keeping well. Hoped they had a good harvest. Sent his love, closed the letter and put it in an envelope, ready for posting.

Jamie borrowed a stamp from Mary and posted his letter, hoping he would get a reply.

It was to be several months before an answer came. Back to school and daily routine for the next couple of weeks. The war was very quiet for now and life went on as usual.

CHAPTER 52

FOREIGN SOLDIERS

It became obvious that America was now in the war. The radio news was full of the arrival of the American GIs. It would not be long before they all became aware of them and the way they were so different to the English and their way of life.

Jamie told Mary that the American soldiers had been seen in Eltham. What did Mary think of that? Mary just shrugged her shoulders, saying, 'We have enough problems without having to worry about them.' Jamie said, 'Surely, they will be a big help to defeat the Germans?' Mary replied, 'I suppose so.'

There were plenty of rumours in school about how they had so much food and didn't know what it was to be hungry. They were giving chewing gum and chocolate bars to children and young women, to make friends. Jamie thought, they are not likely to come here to Welling, so he put them from his mind.

Children were going to sit the half term tests. Jamie asked Harry, 'Why do we have to sit exams? There isn't a school bigger than the secondary modern school I attend. I will never get to grammar school or university. Absolutely no chance." Harry said, 'Just try, son. Just try.'

Jamie told his parents he wanted to learn the German language at school. Did they mind? Harry wanted to know why. Jamie told him, 'We have to learn a foreign language: French or German.' Harry just said, 'OK, son.'

The year was moving rapidly towards July and they would break up for the summer holiday soon, after the tests.

Tests done with until the end of term, Jamie would be on holiday with nowhere to go except the park and the garden.

CHAPTER 53

WAR NEWS

Because the raids on England were now few and far between, everyone was expecting a renewal of the Blitz.

Jamie went to school as usual, now that everything was quiet on the war front in England. News on the radio was several weeks old and mainly about the Japanese conquests in the Far East. However, news had come through that General Rommel had driven the English forces out of the main harbour of Tobruck on the 21st June, which was the worst news they could have had. Jamie asked, 'How could this have happened?' Harry's reply was, 'Probably with the use of ground forces, tanks and dive bombers.'

News was always scarce and at least a week old during wartime. The one thing that was constant was the queueing for food and fuel, which was also scarce. The USA were sending hundreds of ships to England under a scheme called Lend Lease. As new courses were being taken, somehow the ships were getting through, bringing much needed supplies to England. Now there were many American troops arriving in the UK. Stories were going around that a lot of women and girls were getting very friendly with the soldiers, as these troops had money to spend and, better still, they had food to give away to the families of these young ladies. What was all the oohing and ahhing about these girls? What was wrong? Mary didn't know how to explain to Jamie, because he was still a youngster. Mary had forgotten that Jamie already knew the facts of life. At school, Jamie was getting on well.

The summer holiday would start at the end of August, which was now only three weeks away. It would end just before Jamie's 11th birthday.

Jamie had been watching a girl for an opportunity to talk to her. Her name was Sylvia. It seemed they were never at the same place at the same time. Jamie was thinking about girls these days. It rather bewildered him, because he hadn't given girls much thought before. It will pass, Jamie thought.

The news about the war was still coming through, although it was always old news. A week or so before, it had been about Japan and the Far East, now it was about North Africa and the newly promoted German Field Marshal, Rommel. He called English soldiers 'Desert Rats.' Jamie was annoyed about this and exclaimed, 'This field marshal, Rommel, called our soldiers rats!' He asked Harry, 'Why is this field marshal calling our men rats?' Harry had no real answer, but he told Jamie that it was used as an insult. Harry then said, 'But we'll see, as rats tend to bite back when cornered.'

The rest of the month carried on with little or no change. Jamie following his old routine, going backwards and forwards to school during the week, queueing up for food with Mary at the weekend.

At last, the summer holiday was upon them and it was time for the schools to close. They would be shut now for six weeks. Jamie would return on the 7th of September.

CHAPTER 54

A BOAT ON THE LAKE

The first week of September 1942 was dry to start with, but soon turned to mixed sunshine and cloud. Jamie, as usual, was listening to the radio news, which was good this time. Germany was too involved with Russia, however they were still very active in the Atlantic against the English convoys and particularly active against the Arctic convoys to Russia. Attacking both by air and submarines, a great many ships were lost in these convoys. The news about the convoys was coming from the few survivors of the attacks.

Jamie was wondering what to do with his time. He had six weeks to fill, when not helping Mary with shopping and queueing up for food. Jamie was looking for a bit of pleasure and leisure.

Close by was the park. Rather large, with a big lake used for boating. As much as Jamie admired this lake, he had an inherent fear of deep water, as he was unable to swim. He wished that his school gave swimming lessons but no. Perhaps it would happen in future years.

Enclosed in the park was an Army Camp 4 and several anti-aircraft batteries. Looking through the wire surround, Jamie could see the guns. He would love to have been able to go on to the camp with the soldiers and be shown how those mighty guns worked, but that wasn't to be.

Later, Jamie met a friend, just lying on the grass enjoying the sun. Jamie joined him, and they talked. Later they decided to go to the lakeside and talked about going rowing on the lake as it was a great day for such an adventure, even though Jamie dreaded the deep water.

They had just enough money and were able to take out a rowing boat. Jamie was nervous, and they had trouble at first getting aboard the boat, but eventually they were settled and underway. They spent most of the afternoon on the lake until it was time to return to the landing dock.

They managed to steer the boat alongside the landing, where Jamie leaned over to take hold of it. As his pal began to stand up, the boat moved away from the landing. Jamie, holding on tight, began to stretch out over the water as the boat moved gently away. Jamie was yelling at the top of his voice for help. The man who did the hiring rushed over to the boat and pulled it in with his boat hook. He was just in time to stop Jamie falling into the water.

The boatman, in an aggressive voice, said to Jamie, 'Have you never been in a boat before?' Jamie stood and looked at him, shaking with fear that he may have fallen into the water and drowned. He said, 'No, and never again, mister, if I can help it.'

Jamie and his pal turned and walked away. As they walked, they looked at each other and burst out laughing, then started to run to the park gates and home.

On arriving home, Mary asked Jamie what his day had been like. Jamie just looked and said, 'Nothing much, Mum. Just went to the park.'

The next day, Jamie and his pal went back to the park and just lay in the sunshine. It was a lovely day, the sun shining, bright blue sky with a gentle breeze blowing. While relaxing on the grassy ground, a shadow was cast across their eyes. Jamie looked up and saw the shape of a girl looking down at them. The girl said, 'Hello, Jamie.' Jamie saw it was Sylvia and felt excited. She was the girl he had wanted to meet for some time, but they had never been close enough to have a chat. Here was the opportunity.

They talked for a while. Jamie's pal lay there, not taking any notice. As they talked, Jamie found out that Sylvia (the girl of his dreams) already had a boyfriend. As she turned and said, 'Bye, Jamie' and walked away, Jamie thought this friendship would go no further and dismissed Sylvia from his mind.

The rest of the day, Jamie and his friend, Jack, just lay on the grass, enjoying the sunshine.

Gradually, the holiday period of six weeks was disappearing and it wouldn't be long now before he would be returning to school on 7th September. It was clear there would be more boys in the class as families were returning from evacuation.

CHAPTER 55

SELF ASSESSMENT

To Jamie, September always had a certain warm feeling. Mornings were misty and strangely quiet. As the mornings warmed up, so the quietness and a gentle breeze seemed present. It was only September that gave Jamie the feeling he loved. Perhaps it was because it was his birth month, which always gave Jamie a feeling of contentment.

Now it was back to school. Jamie would have loved to have been in the fields for harvest, then hay making, with that hot, sticky feeling, with seeds and grass sticking to sweat, making you look dusty and feel very dry, getting hungry from hard work. But no, it was a stuffy classroom instead.

As usual, the radio news came through at two weeks old. In the Far East, the Japanese had over-run most of the pacific islands. There was, however, good news from Africa.

On the African front, at the battle of El Alamein, the English army had pushed Rommel out of Alamein. England had won a great battle. Jamie was pleased as punch for the army. At last, there was some good news in beating the enemy.

On the 7th, everyone returned to school, but it made Jamie wish he had more time off. He didn't want to go back. Then it occurred to Jamie that next week, as they had been reminded, was Battle of Britain Day, as Mr Churchill had named it, on the 15th. Jamie would have his 11th birthday on the same day. It also reminded Jamie that there were now only three years left of schooling and he would have to start thinking about his future when he left school at the age of 14. Jamie wondered, what work was he good for? He wasn't good at carpentry, not too good at metalwork. He was no athlete, nor a teacher. Clerical work was OK, and his maths wasn't too bad. He thought about farming, but no, that was too much like hard work, as much as he had enjoyed it. Shop work, perhaps? Jamie thought, blow it, I'll make my decision later, nearer the time.

The next bit of war news came: the German troops had repelled the British landing in a place called Dieppe on the French coast and for the commandos, it had been an absolute disaster. Many had been captured and many, unfortunately, were killed. Although they had beaten England at Dieppe, the Russians at Stalingrad had brought the German army to a standstill. Then the radio told of a reversal in Africa. Rommel had renewed their advance on Africa to El Alamein. It was announced that, in North Africa again, the desert rats held the German advance and remained in control of El Alamein.

That evening at teatime, Jamie was full of the news that the British had held on to where they were in El Alamein and had repelled Rommel and his Afrika Korps again. Harry said to Jamie, 'The desert rats bit back, at long last.'

CHAPTER 56

JAMIE'S BIKE 1942

Late in September, Harry was making his way home after work in the dark. There were no street lights and you were only allowed a shielded torch. Passing one open shop, Harry noticed it was a new shop with a lot of what appeared to be recovered articles. On its list of things for sale was a bicycle, priced three pounds. Thinking about Jamie's birthday, Harry went in, talked to the owner, then put ten shillings on the bike for him to hold until the 14th.

Harry told Mary that evening about the bike. Mary asked if they could really afford it. Harry said, 'We haven't been able to give our son very much. I think we should, but I will only buy it if you agree.' Mary agreed and said, 'My little teapot should keep us for a week.'

Harry got his pay on Friday, as normal, and made his way to the shop. He paid for the bike and started wheeling it home. This was going to be a big surprise for Jamie. Harry decided to take a note of the frame number, go to the police station and check that it hadn't been reported as stolen. Harry was told it would take a while to check and agreed to wait ten days.

One evening, there was a knock on the door. When Harry opened it, it was a policeman with the message that the bike had not been stolen. It was clear and good luck. Then he was gone.

Now Harry could reveal his and Mary's secret to Jamie.

The next evening, when Harry came home, he took Jamie out to the shed in the garden and told Jamie to go in. There was yell of delight. Jamie came rushing out and flung his arms around Harry. It was then that Mary told Jamie to be careful, as Jamie was considerably bigger than Harry and she was worried that Harry might get hurt by Jamie's enthusiasm. Jamie was both laughing and crying with joy. Eventually, he settled down, as he realised he couldn't ride a bike yet and had to learn.

That evening, Mary and Harry talked about what they would do for Steven, to make things fair. He had shown interest in a tricycle he had seen in a book. It could wait until Christmas, if Harry could find one.

Jamie said he, too, would look around, and if he found one, he'd let them know.

CHAPTER 57

RELIEF OF MALTA

The weather was cold, dry and overcast in London, as it had been for several weeks. Now Mary had to light a fire to keep the house warm, using their precious fuel. Young Steven needed to be kept reasonably warm.

There were still air raids every so often, but they were sporadic. The radio news was saying how, for many months, a little island in the Mediterranean, called Malta, had been under attack daily by the German Luftwaffer but it had withstood the siege. Now it was announced that the island, at last, was no longer under siege. The RAF had received new Spitfires and could now defend the island against the attacking German planes. Now ships laden with supplies were at last reaching the island. English aircraft were attacking enemy shipping going to Africa. By stopping enemy supplies reaching the Africa Korps, England was stopping Rommel's forces in the desert. They were running out of petrol, disabling Rommel's tanks.

Jamie, of course, asked the usual questions about Malta, both at school and of Harry. In geography, the teacher tried to explain why the island was so important. It was between Italy and North Africa. Germany needed to use the Italian ports to supply the Afrika Korps in Africa. The German field marshal, Rommel, was being driven back from Al Alamein because of the lack of military supplies and petrol for his tanks.

Two days later, it was reported that Free French forces had stopped fighting, as the Allies had captured Tunisia, where their army was stationed. For Jamie, it seemed that, at long last, the Allied forces were beginning to get the upper hand, if all the news was true.

CHAPTER 58

COLDS CLOSE SCHOOLS

December 1942 dawned with a damp, cold morning and for the first two weeks, it was much the same.

On Christmas Day, the weather turned extremely cold, followed by wet and misty days and very much colder. The trouble was, although it was cold, food was still scarce. Fuel was also scarce, which Mary needed to keep the family warm and lessen the chance of colds. Mary was worried about young Steven, who had developed a bad head cold. She had difficulty keeping the house warm, but she kept Steven wrapped in clothes and as warm as possible. There was little or no medicine to help with the bad cough that Steven had. Mary made up her onion-based cough medicine. Steven was not to be the only one with a bad cold; Jamie went down with it just the same, and was kept home from school. It seemed that the same cold was running through all the school children. It was a winter 'flu-like cold. Mary went out each day to find onions and, if possible, sugar or honey. Harry was still well, at least. He didn't have the cold. Mary to managed to stay well, too.

Jamie tried to keep up with his education at home, but with the cold and the cough, the bad nights and the headaches, he wasn't doing well.

On Christmas Day, Mary worked her magic by cooking the rabbit with as many vegetables as were available. It was not as big as usual, the rabbit, but was enough for all to have a reasonable dinner. Harry said grace and thanked God for his help.

Later, Mary made a soup from the remains of the rabbit, for both Jamie and Steven. Just like last Christmas, it was a day much like any other day: no decorations and very quiet. Jamie listened to the radio but Harry was concerned about the battery running low. Jamie was restricted to a couple of radio stories and the news, but there wasn't a great deal of news on the radio about what was going on in North Africa, the Far East, or even the Russian front, except that Stalingrad was no longer in the state of siege. The Russian winter had started and heavy snow was affecting the German army. Their men had started to retreat. Jamie had learnt that Russian winters were extremely cold, far colder than anything that could come about in the UK. Jamie tried to imagine what it would be like, forty degrees below freezing. He could not imagine how cold that was.

The local weather did not improve for the rest of the month. Now there was snow falling and Mary would not let Jamie, with his cold, go outside.

CHAPTER 59

NEW YEAR 1943

The New Year started with heavy snow and sleet, with a strong northerly wind driving the weather. By the third week, the snow was causing havoc in the north of the country, with many snow-drifts. London was also having traffic problems, with both snow and army traffic. This was primarily due to wet snow being frozen solid during the night time frosts, making movement difficult. Jamie had trouble, every morning, walking to the school, because the pavements were so slippery with ice. His bicycle was of no use in this weather. At school, during playtime, the boys made slides in the playground. The teacher quoted: 'Boys will be boys.' The classrooms were extremely cold as there was no fuel for the boiler to be turned on. The boys wore their gloves and topcoats in the classroom to keep warm. The gloves made writing extremely dif-ficult. At the end of the day, everybody went home, hoping that there was a fire in the grate.

The Americans had been arriving in great numbers for the last few months and created large military camps in the UK. They were gathered into a mighty force with bigger and better bomber aircraft. There were items of gossip from many sources, which included some from the USAF boys in pubs, passed on by word of mouth. It was this news that Jamie listed in the diary he had tried to keep since returning from evacuation.

There was little news on the radio concerning the war, except that Stalingrad was continuing to fight. England was sending arms and ammunition to Russia, helping them to build their armies with equipment, to enable them to make war against the German occupation themselves.

The convoys crossing the Arctic Ocean suffered many attacks from submarines, which formed what was called 'wolf packs'.

England lost many ships and many men on these convoys. The news about the convoys was only released to the public once Russia was in a position to look after her own part of the war. For Jamie, it was old news by many weeks, but he kept a note of it all.

January gradually moved into February and the weather had not changed at all. It was still cold, with a cold wind blowing, and Jamie was still having to go to school in the early mornings in the dark. Jamie had no choice.

CHAPTER 60

GOOD NEWS FOR UK

School kept everybody busy now. Making use of the hall every morning for exercise, it had been turned into a gymnasium. Jamie was never very keen on this sort of exercise but found that he was better at most of the exercises than he thought. He could not scale a rope, however much he tried. Jamie had been thinking of trying to find a small job that would give him pocket money, same as when he was with Mr Wilson, but because most of the jobs were either in the very early morning, such as a paper delivery round, Mary had said, 'No. It is too dangerous in the dark.' It seemed that Mary had forgotten about Jamie's rabbit snare clearance round in the early mornings at the farm and how dark it had been then. It was different in the towns.

Every evening, Jamie listened to the radio and made notes in his diary.

The bad weather had continued throughout January, and February was only a little better. March was on its way, with high winds. The weather was just a little better. The frosts just didn't last as long. Although it was still cold, there was no snow to freeze over at night.

Going to school every morning, Jamie never looked forward to the exercise session as it always made him hungry and he would have to wait until midday before he could have his sandwich.

March was moving on. The news reported that the RAF had bombed the town of Essen. It had destroyed most of the town, mainly Krupp's munitions factory. The raid must have been successful. The RAF had no losses to their bombers.

It was a Saturday and Jamie was sitting on part of a wall in the foundations of the bombsite next door. He was just musing about school and things that had happened since leaving the farm

131

and how life had changed so much, looking around the site. Although it was still chilly, Jamie didn't mind, as a new spring was on its way. He noticed some green shoots around the edge of the bomb crater. Jamie went for a closer inspection, to find that the shoots looked as if they were flower shoots. Jamie just had to tell Mary of his find, and ask if she wanted him to dig them up. Mary told Jamie to leave them, as they must have been in the garden before the bomb and they had survived.

On the radio, there was news about a large raid on a town in Germany called Wilhelmhaven; a very large port where a lot of damage had been done.

March moved into April. It was now obvious that spring was underway. The month of April started with showery weather, which lasted for a couple of weeks, then it gradually turned fine. It was then that news came of a massive Russian counterattack over the town of Stalingrad, breaking the siege which had raged for months. Now the Russians had defeated the German army and were driving them back. Jamie heard, from a friend at school, that in the cinema, there was a Pathé news reel film about the English victory in the desert against the German Afrika Korps, also about the Russian victory. Jamie wanted to see it, but he needed his father to take him, because, under the age of 16, he was not allowed into a cinema on his own. But no luck. Harry did not want to go, nor could he easily afford it.

A few days passed and Jamie was, again, on the bombsite, just sitting on the same wall in the ruined foundation of the bombed house next door, scanning the site. Although he had done this many times before, he had never taken in what was happening on the site. He was looking at the crater of the bomb and noticed that there were many more larger green shoots coming up all around the edge of the bomb crater; much more than the last time he had looked. Curiosity made Jamie get up and go for a closer look at these plant shoots. He was surprised at the amount of flower shoots. His time on the farm kicked him into gear. He thought they looked like bluebells, in little clumps, here and there. Also, there were long shoots which looked very much like daffodil leaves, just a few; one here, one there. There were primulas as well, right on the edge of the slope, going down to the base of the crater, the waterline. Jamie was so impressed that he ran into the house to tell Mary what he had found. Jamie asked if she would like him to dig them up for their garden. Mary sighed and said, 'No, son. Leave them there. We need veggies, not flowers. We will see the beauty of them from our own garden.'

On the radio that night, there was a report that there had been a major air raid on Aberdeen in Scotland. There had been a lot of damage and many casualties. Also England had lost several more ships, sunk by German U-boats.

Jamie's schooling had progressed, but he remained in the B classes. Now he was looking forward to the May bank holiday break. He could then get on with gardening, ready for planting vegetables for the rest of the year. It wouldn't take as long as before.

Jamie quickly had the ground turned and ready for planting. Tired, he slept very well that night, with no disturbance; not even the sound of aircraft flying overhead.

CHAPTER 61

THE RETURNING

Now that May had arrived, it seemed to Jamie that his world had changed so much, since returning from evacuation, that he hardly recognised it, and it was still changing. More and more children were returning from wherever they had been sent. More and more boys were filling the classroom. The talk in the classroom was sounding almost foreign as there were so many different dialects but it was still English and in time they mostly slipped back into southern-style speech.

Jamie had made few friends during his time in school, unlike most of the others, who had formed groups. Jamie had just three friends with whom he spent most of his free time.

Jamie spent some time at home checking on the progress of the plants he had discovered. They seemed to be growing well. Now there were lupins clearly showing their green tops. The weed, bellbind, was growing up the little bit of fencing very quickly. Brambles were also growing and not only on the bombsite but in the alleyways. This meant that there would be blackberries later in the year.

That evening, on the radio, the newsreader said that it was snowing in Scotland and Wales, but in Kent, it was clear and warm. Jamie thought, how strange to have snow in May, and he hoped it didn't come to the south. Jamie was brought sharply back to reality at the sound of a lot of heavy bombers flying overhead, bound for Germany. Jamie hoped they would all return safely but he knew that this was most unlikely. There were always some losses.

For the first few days, the weather was overcast, with light rain. Later, as the skies cleared, the only aircraft were England's own; mainly USAF bombers flying out towards Germany. Jamie thought, this must be good for the English airmen as it must be giving them a time to rest.

It was now two hours ahead of Greenwich Mean Time, which meant that it was light until 10pm. This was primarily to help the farms with their production of food. Jamie had followed the farmers' lead and planted vegetables early in the year. Both front and back gardens looked to be flourishing. On the bombsite, where Jamie had noticed all the new shoots and, on examination, found them to be flowers coming into bud, the bluebells were in bloom, much to Mary's delight. It looked quite amazing as they brightened up the bombsite.

England was now awash with American forces. Most of the aircraft seen during the day were USAF heavy bombers leaving in mass, almost too many to count, to bomb Germany. Every evening, Jamie heard them pass overhead and prayed that they would return home safely.

On the 18th June, on the radio news, it was reported that the Royal Air Force had successfully bombed and broken the Mohne and Ada, two major dams in Germany. There had been several planes lost but they had successfully burst the dams and the flooding had caused much damage, destroying factories in the Ruhr Valley. Harry, Mary, Jamie and young Steven, as they ate dinner, heard this news and it caused much conversation at the dinner table. Jamie wanted to know, was it a good idea, on England's part, to flood such a large valley? Harry responded, 'Yes, anything that destroys factories in Germany is good.'

Shortly after the news had finished, there was a radio story. Jamie spent the early evening listening to it. Later, sitting quietly, he thought of his friend Roy and that he hadn't written for some time. He must write to him soon.

At school, although there were a lot more boys, attendance was not strictly adhered to, as many mothers kept their children at home, regardless of any school rules. Mary, however, insisted that Jamie went to school every day that it was open.

Now the news coming through was about the Russian front. The Russian army was now forcing the German army to retreat.

The weeks passed and June moved into July. The weather was sunny and dry, allowing Jamie to get out and go to the park in the evenings, as there was still some time before dark. If he wasn't going out to the park, either to meet a friend or just wandering on his own, then he had to work on the gardens, front and back.

Harry was busy at work. He could not explain to Jamie exactly what was being built but Jamie had heard the name 'Bailey' and it turned out to be a Bailey bridge, which was a mobile bridge that could be built over a river by the Royal Engineers. At that time, neither Harry nor Jamie, nor anyone in the civilian world, even knew what these were or that they were even being made.

CHAPTER 62

A NASTY SHOCK

The days were warm and sunny as July came in. Harry and Jamie were in the garden. Jamie asked Harry if Mum had got any late potato seeds. After few minutes, there was no answer. Jamie turned and found Harry sitting on the ground, clasping his leg. Harry told Jamie to get Mary as he needed help. Mary arrived and Jamie was already running down the road towards the doctors. On arriving at the surgery, gasping for air, he managed to tell the nurse what had happened. Harry needed help. The nurse went into the doctor's office and Jamie took off running back home. As he arrived, he found Mary sitting on the ground with Harry. Harry couldn't get up.

About ten minutes later, the doctor arrived on his bicycle. He quickly looked at Harry's leg then looked up and told Jamie to go to the telephone at the end of the road and phone for an ambulance.

Twenty-five minutes later it arrived, bell clanging loudly. They quickly got Harry onto a stretcher and put him into the ambulance. Harry was taken to Brook Hospital, along with Mary.

Jamie went indoors, collected Steven, and they sat and waited. Steven was full of questions. He was nearly five, now. Jamie calmed himself and Steven by cuddling him.

Mary waited at the hospital. It was some time before a doctor could inform Mary that Harry would be kept in until he was fit to go home and gave Mary assurance that he would be OK after a rest and some new medication. Mary explained that she had no medical insurance and, on previous occasions, the AFS had paid for Harry's medical care. The doctor told her not to worry and to get off home and rest.

When Mary got home, she found Steven and Jamie asleep on the sofa together, Steven in Jamie's arms. She gently took Steven to bed. Returning, she found Jamie awake and told him to go to bed. She said she would tell him what had happened in the morning.

Next morning, as Jamie and Steven were sitting down to breakfast, Mary told them that Harry would be staying in hospital for a short while. He had cut his leg on something sharp at work. Like most men, he had thought nothing of it and didn't have it seen to. As a result, it had become infected, and needed to be attended to before it became too serious. He was OK, just needed to rest for a while. She was going to visit him shortly. They would have to stay at Gran and Grandad's house if she was home late, then she would collect them.

CHAPTER 63

BREAKTHROUGH

July moved into August. The weather remained warm and humid. That evening, Jamie spent some time listening to the radio, without learning anything new.

The next morning was nice and sunny. Jamie thought, I've got no more work to do in the gardens. It's all finished, except for harvesting the fruit and veg. Jamie now had to think of school. He started with some homework revision, as he would have to return to school in seven days, on the 7th September, as the summer holidays were over in two weeks. He would have his 13th birthday and would have to prepare to leave next year.

Jamie felt that he didn't really want to go back to school. He should really be deciding what work to look for. There didn't seem to be anyone who could advise him.

As Jamie was lying there, in the sunshine, doing his homework, the siren sounded. People, including Jamie, had got rather complacent and didn't take much notice of the siren. Jamie was looking up and couldn't see anything but could hear a lone plane up there. It sounded like a Spitfire, somewhere. Jamie wondered why he was stooging around; there wasn't any other aircraft up there. Nothing unusual happened and Jamie made his way home, as Mary should be there, making tea.

The next day, Mary arrived home with the news that Harry was making good progress and, with just another couple of weeks spent resting, should be returning home. It would be some time before he could return to work, though.

On the 7th September, Jamie returned to school. He didn't particularly want to this year but he wanted to meet one or two of his friends, as he was feeling just a bit lonely. His friend, Will, didn't turn up and no one seemed to know what had happened.

On the 15th, Jamie's birthday, he was told that William would not be returning to school as he'd developed a rather nasty illness which had left him unable to speak and paralysed down one side. Jamie felt even lower because Will was a very good friend. He must try and find out if he could visit sometime.

Jamie's Birthday was a very quiet day. He had received a card from his mum and dad and a little picture on a card with 'happy birthday' printed on it from Steven. This was his 13th birthday, leaving just one year before he left school and had to go to work and earn a living.

At home, now, in the second week of September, most of the vegetables in the garden were ready to be lifted and the fruit had to be picked soon before the birds ate it. The fruit would be needed at home during the cold winter months. Mary would be busy preserving and storing all the produce the garden had made.

Gradually the month moved into October.

CHAPTER 64

JAMIE'S WORRY

Jamie felt pleased with the fact that he had picked and saved all the fruit and vegetables from the garden. On the weekends, Mary managed to preserve the fruit and dry store the vegetables.

The weather had become colder and, Jamie had thought, if he had left it any longer there would have been a considerable loss. All his hard work would have been for nothing. Jamie had little to do now. It was all down to Mary. He had to think about finding a job.

He spent the morning cleaning out the rabbit hutch and putting in fresh straw. It occurred to him that, perhaps next year, if they had another rabbit, it might be OK to let her have a litter. That is, if it was a 'her'.

Late that afternoon, Mary and Steven arrived home from shopping. Mary had a smile on her face as she told Jamie and Harry that she had found a school place for Steven. The school was in Welling and he would start in January. Mary told Jamie that Harry would be able to return to work now that his leg was better but he would still have to take life slowly for a while and he would have to take his tablets regularly until the infection was completely gone. 'We must keep an eye on him for a little while.'

After a couple of days, life started to settle down to a routine, with Mary looking after the home, Harry spending time with Steven and Jamie going back to school. Now it was time to stock up on fuel, so Jamie and Mary were, again, in the queue for winter coal and also for whatever food was available to add to their own produce.

The weather was changeable and, when going out to stand in a queue, they needed to put on a topcoat, regardless. Sometimes they could stand for more than half an hour, just to get to the front and find that the shop had sold out.

Jamie wanted to leave school and find work to help the family, but the law said he had to stay until his 14th birthday. He spoke to Harry and Mary about getting work and they both said yes, but not by leaving school.

Jamie started looking in the local shop windows for the phrase, 'Boy wanted.' He finally found a paper round, starting at 6am, before school. For this, he would be paid five shillings per week.

It was hard going, for a week. The early morning frosts and the cold winds made the start difficult, but Jamie got used to it. He quickly became one of the boys and made friends with the others.

On his first payday, he gave Mary his pay envelope. She took four shillings out and gave Jamie just the one, which he put in his old money box from Mrs Wilson.

There was a lull in the air raids and bombings, which was fine. It meant that a good night's sleep could be had.

CHAPTER 65

ANOTHER WINTER

Gradually the month moved into November. The weather turned colder and there was need of a fire. At least there was a little more food in the shops but no change with shopping and queueing most of the day on Saturdays. As usual, Jamie and Mary went to the shops to collect their meagre ration allowances of butter, cheese and meat. Jamie's newspaper round only brought in five shillings a week. The four shillings Jamie gave to Mary each week helped. Harry's wage was three pounds a week, which was now the main income. Mary worked part time for two half-days a week, which paid one pound ten shillings a week and this helped to run the house. The rabbit would be eaten but on New Year's Day as Mary had managed to order a chicken. This would be a rare delight. They had not had chicken since leaving the farm. It was going to be the best Christmas dinner for several years. Christmas this year was also looking like it was going to be the safest.

There was more food available in the shops but fuel was still short and needed queuing for, as normal. Many more ships were arriving safely with goods from abroad.

Jamie had been saving shillings for weeks and felt that his money could buy at least a present for Steven; a small present.

There were still seven weeks until Christmas. Although it was mild during the day, there were frosts every morning. Jamie felt the frost as he was out delivering papers at 6am until 7:45am then home for breakfast and off to school.

Jamie had a very busy life. Sometimes he wondered if there was ever going to be something different.

Just before Christmas, it was announced that boys of eighteen had to register for conscription into the coal mines. They were to be called 'Bevin Boys'. What would it be like, when the war finally

143

ended? Recently, on the home front, it had been quiet, with no German aircraft in the sky and little or no sirens.

The war news was coming in. It was about North Africa as the UK forces were getting the upper hand against the Italians and the Africka Korps.

At school, Jamie's work was improving because he had not spent time working at home. Now it was approaching the end of year examinations. Mary and Harry were quite happy with Jamie's progress.

The month was now moving on rapidly and thoughts were turning to Christmas. Jamie had savings, but what to purchase for a Christmas present for his brother, Steven?

It looked like it was going to be a much better Christmas. Perhaps now the family could all look forward to 1944.

CHAPTER 66

CHRISTMAS AND GOOD WILL

December 1943 dawned dry and chilly with infrequent showers. Jamie was looking forward to Christmas Day, even though it looked like there would be very little in the way of gifts. Some of his savings he had given to Mary, to get something for young Steven. Harry was looking much better as he was occupied at work and he now didn't have the worries that he had had over the last year. No more problems, as his leg had healed.

Christmas Day found Jamie helping Mary however he could. Jamie sat at the kitchen table, peeling potatoes and shucking peas. He then prepared the few parsnips and greens, all the time talking to Mary as she prepared the chicken she had managed to buy, then put in the oven to roast. Steven was playing in the living room and Harry was reading a book.

They all sat down about 2pm and had Christmas dinner. Mary had made a fruit pie for their sweet, with the cream from the top of the milk. Dinner was fine, better than any of them expected. Steven showed delight at getting a Christmas present, a small, toy, three-wheeled pedal bike, not new, but refurbished. It looked good and was from Mary and Harry. Jamie's gift was a pencil box with all the pieces inside ready for schooldays after Christmas.

Jamie went into the kitchen and insisted on doing the washing up while Mary sat with Harry and Steven. As usual, at 3pm, the radio was turned on and the King's speech was listened to in silence.

Shortly afterwards, Jamie said he was going for a walk in the park. It started to get late and he hadn't returned. Mary was worried, as there was no street lighting. Then Jamie came in, just in time for his evening tea. He sat but said nothing of his walk. As usual, the radio was turned on for the news, then Christmas music was played, but because of the battery running low, the radio was turned off.

That evening, Jamie talked with Harry about what had been on his mind all day and asked for some guidance about the work he should consider. Jamie would be leaving school in a little over eight months and had no idea what he wanted to do. The talk was no help as Harry had always worked in an iron yard and now in an office and had no idea about other types of work, but he did tell Jamie that people always needed shoemakers, undertakers and shop workers. Jamie thought he would have to talk with his teacher from now on.

On New Year's Day 1944, Jamie didn't feel very much like doing anything and just sat drawing or reading. He felt he wanted to be quiet. Both Mary and Harry asked if he was alright. Jamie said he was, then stayed very quiet for the rest of the day until bedtime. He slept well but woke up feeling tired. He had had the strangest of dreams about girls.

CHAPTER 67

A BRIGHTER LOOK TO 1944

Sitting at the breakfast table, looking at his mother and brother, everything was strangely still and quiet. Suddenly, Jamie felt quite strange and started to shake. He tried to stand but collapsed on the floor and blacked out.

It was some time later that Jamie became aware that he was in bed and there was a strange face leaning over him. The face belonged to the doctor. It turned away and spoke. Jamie heard him say, 'Mrs, the lad must rest. I don't know what he's been doing but he is exhausted. I think you should know, he is becoming a man. Has his voice broken yet? Let him rest for the next few days. I will come back tomorrow. Give him plenty of water and let him sleep. Goodnight.' Then he left.

It was some twelve hours later that Jamie awoke. When he tried to call Mary, his voice was croaky. Jamie was thinking, I must get up for my paper round. Mary soon put a stop to that, making him stay in bed. She told him his Aunt Lil would be coming while he was resting, as she had to go out.

Aunt Lil arrived and took over from Mary. Jamie lay back, letting his mind roam over all that had happened over the last four years. When would all this end? Was the war still going well for England? He gave in and fell asleep.

Later that day, the doctor came and talked to Jamie about the changes his body was beginning to go through. These changes would make him into a man. He would have some strange feelings in his private parts, but this was normal, and he would soon adapt. His voice would become deeper and he would probably not want his mother to see him naked. Jamie, with all this turning over in his mind, was reminded that he must carry on with his schooling until September, then he would have to leave. He could still help his mum, things would be OK. He could go back to school in the next couple of weeks.

It was at the end of January that Mary allowed Jamie to return to school, even though the weather was mild, with frequent rain showers and heavy clouds which could easily turn to snow. Jamie made his way to school every morning, looking forward to the lessons he had missed.

There were frequent bombing raids. The news on the radio told of an increase of U-boat activity in the Artic, sinking more English ships. Then came the shocking news that a school in Catford in south-east London had been bombed and forty children had died.

Slowly the month moved on to February. It was very cold for the first two weeks. Jamie was able to go to school and the school itself now had some form of heating. It was only in the second and third week of the month that the weather turned much colder and there were snow showers across England. It looked as though it would carry on into March.

More food ships were coming into the country. They had more protection and were getting through to the docks. Things felt a little easier and everybody was relaxing and getting on with going to work, producing war material.

March arrived. The weather turned exceptionally dry but in Scotland there was very heavy snowfall. The snow moved south into the north of England but when the weather front arrived in the south, it had turned to rain.

In the south, the air raids had more or less stopped. The army had a new anti-aircraft gun that fired rockets. On the first occasion, when it was test fired, the sound of the rockets caused panic and people rushed to get into the subway in Bethnal Green. There was a major accident and over a hundred people were killed or injured in the terrible fall and crush.

Now there was rain in the south and the trees showed that spring was on the way. The trees had got their buds and the grass was green, although the ground was soggy.

March moved on with very little change, also very little changed in the way of war news. There was little on the news about what was happening anywhere in the world. It was like there was a blackout of news. It was just a miserable time because of the bad weather.

March slowly but surely moved into April. The rain returned as frequent showers throughout the month. The plants were doing exceedingly well as spring was here at last.

May came in drier and warmer. Sunshine was breaking through and the ground was drying out. Gradually the weather changed to wet with a strong wind blowing across the south-east. London was inundated with rain and wind. Jamie said to Mary, 'Mum, it looks like the farmers are gonna have a bad harvest this year due to late planting. They should have done it last month. I'm sure Mr Wilson must be worried. What do you think, Mum?' Mary replied, 'Son, the weather is something we have no control over whatsoever. We just have to live with it and put up with it. Get ready for school, as I now have to think about finding someone to take your brother. He's five now, hasn't time gone fast?'

CHAPTER 68

BEGINNING OF THE END

May moved into June and Jamie found that going to school wasn't very pleasant with the rain and the wind blowing hard. Jamie had no choice; he had to go to school. At least school was warm. He met a few friends, as usual, on the way. They talked about this and that, how the bombing raids had stopped and that they had the feeling a better time was coming.

It was the end of the first week and there was noise in the air on this fine day. There were a lot of bombers flying overhead heading towards France. Most of the boys stood in the playground and watched as they flew. Jamie, like the rest of the boys at school, was surprised, wondering just what was happening.

Several days later, it was announced on the radio that England, along with America, had successfully landed their armies in Cherbourg, France. The air force had made heavy bombing raids all along the Cherbourg coast in support of the invasion. Then came the news that the Russians were advancing into Poland, pushing closer to Germany's borders. Jamie, not for the first time, felt that this perhaps was the beginning of England's winning streak. There was the feeling that England had started the beginning of the end of World War Two. Jamie of course knew that it wasn't over yet but hopefully it would be soon.

In the first week of June there was a lull in the weather. On the morning of the 6th, the air was full of planes flying towards France. Jamie had stood with his mates, watching the bombers flying to France.

The radio news was unusually quiet. Jamie said his usual prayer for the flyers, hoping they all returned safely. He then went back into class, where he spent the rest of the day.

It was one week later, when Jamie and a friend were walking to school, that they heard a strange sound, not unlike a motorbike, coming from the sky. They stopped and looked up, to see a strange-looking aircraft. It looked like a dart but with short, stubby wings and had fire flaming from its tail. They said together, 'It's on fire!' and watched as it flew onwards towards central London. Neither of them knew it was a flying bomb, a V1.

That evening, at last, the news broke that the Allies had invaded France and had successfully landed their troops in five different places at a place called Cherbourg.

The V1s were coming fast; about a hundred a day. Jamie said to Harry that evening after dinner, 'I thought the war was about to end?' Harry replied, "Not for a while yet, son.' Shortly after that, the news reported that English troops were moving inland, but the V1s just kept coming, doing a great deal of damage and causing many casualties. Everyone was hoping that the army would manage to stop them.

CHAPTER 69

THE ALLIES PUSH FORWARD

The rest of the June 1944 weather was much the same.

The news was much better: now the Allies were pushing eastwards towards Germany, trying to reach the bridges to cross the Rhine river. Once across, they could push right into the heart of Germany.

The news from an American news reporter on the radio was that the English troops had been involved in a battle for one of the main bridges in Holland at a place called Arnhem. Sadly, after nine days, the forces had to withdraw. England had not been able to secure the bridge. It had been costly and a big disappointment.

At home, things had quietened. The V1 buzz bombs had finished as the advancing army made them move further back, and the RAF had bombed a place called Dresden and created a fire storm, killing thousands of people, who had been sucked into the storm.

On 8th September, there was an explosion in London which was reported as a gas leak, but after the second, it was discovered that it was a new German weapon; a rocket called a V2. These rockets gave no warning, they just crashed and exploded, killing whoever was in that area. They blew down whole streets of terraced houses. They were terrifying. Jamie, along with his friend, was blown over on his way to school by a blast wave, but neither were injured.

Jamie told his friend, 'This is my final week. Next week I leave school and I must find work.' Ben, his friend, asked, 'What are you going to do?' Jamie shrugged his shoulders and said, 'I haven't the faintest idea.'

That evening, on the news, it was reported that American forces were surrounded at a place in Belgium called Bastogne, as a

German surprise attack at a place called the Ardennes had pushed the American troops back until they made a stand. The Battle of the Bulge was to become the name of this battle and it was bogged down with bad weather. Jamie took note of all this information as it was released, to keep his diary up to date.

Many more boys had returned home from evacuation. The school was filling up. Classes were much larger, up from ten or twelve to thirty boys per class. There was a great deal of lesson review to bring some of the newcomers up to date. Sometimes the lesson got lost on the way as the teachers had come out of retirement and the boys asked a lot of questions they could not answer.

October was a miserable month weather-wise. It rained day after day, with a very cold wind. The bad weather didn't help with queuing for home supplies. It was among the worst things that had to be done; standing in the cold wind and rain that gave many people winter colds, and the elderly were the worst sufferers.

Jamie said to Harry one evening, 'Dad, this is now like peacetime. Was it always like this?' Harry just laughed, shook his head and said, 'No, son. It was worse.'

November didn't change, with just one exception; it got even wetter and just as cold, with light snow flurries.

Now little Steven was at a school for infants, situated in Hook Lane, Welling, Kent. Mary had to take him every morning and, at roughly 3pm, Jamie went and collected him from school.

Steven was growing up. He was nearly six and still had boyish ways. Jamie thought he was wonderful. He really did love this little boy and hoped he had a good life ahead. Of course, he would be able to help him, as he was seven years older. He was his big brother.

There was little change in the weather, it just got colder and foggy.

December 1944 came in wet and with a pea soup fog. The news said that it was snowing in Scotland, causing great disruption. All the time the heavy fog was over London, there was no possibility of air raids of any description.

London, too, was almost at a standstill as far as traffic was concerned, which had increased with the military vehicles trying to get from A to B. In that weather, it was really very slow, and very difficult.

Jamie's diary had very little war news over October, November and December, as there was little or no news on the radio, except about the Americans who were still surrounded but holding in Bastogne.

CHAPTER 70

CHRISTMAS 1944

December. No change. It was wet, foggy and very cold. There were clothes in the shops but getting anything depended on the coupons given out for clothes and many other things, like sweets, meat and dairy produce. This made it a little hard to buy Christmas presents by way of clothing for the cold weather.

Mary had joined a Christmas club in which she paid a florin a week. This would pay out all she had paid in, in time for Christmas, which made it possible to buy a large chicken for Christmas dinner. Jamie thought, this might just be the best Christmas for five long years. Harry had also joined one of these clubs, therefore he had a good amount of money to collect also. This year, Jamie had no money of his own, as Mary had stopped his paper round when he was unwell earlier in the year. He was at a loss for what he could do for Mary, Harry and Steven.

Jamie set about making Christmas cards for them all. He would have them completed just in time for Christmas morning, in just two weeks.

The two weeks passed quickly. Steven's school had closed for the festive holiday period, Jamie had completed his cards and was ready for Christmas Day. Even the overcoats on the bed didn't keep the heat in. Jamie's parents had money in their pockets for the first time in the last three years. Jamie was happy for them. They all sat down together at 3pm and listened to the King's speech, then tucked in to a roast chicken dinner and a small Christmas pudding with the cream off the milk.

After dinner and the King's speech, Harry gave Jamie a small parcel from him and Mary. Jamie opened it and found a scarf, gloves, a diary and an envelope. In the envelope was a pound note, as well as a note saying, 'This is the place to go to for your first job interview and the fare to get there. Good luck, son! Love Mum and Dad.' Jamie thought how wonderful it was.

Harry didn't let Jamie listen to the news that night but insisted on playing music on the old record player and himself playing the piano. The piano had stood in the corner of the living room since they had been given the place to live. It was well out of tune but Harry played it anyway. Both items belonged to the owner of the house, who was living abroad.

Three days passed and now it was New Year's Day 1945. Jamie asked Harry what he thought this year would bring. Harry thought that there would be change, but what, he had no idea.

There had been little war news over the last few days.

CHAPTER 71

THE FINAL PUSH, 1945

The January weather had come in cold. There was a very thick frost and heavy snow bringing more difficulties to the people, who were trying to keep warm and fed.

As the month moved on, the weather changed and turned warmer, causing the thaw to set in, then it turned to rain.

Jamie made an appointment with the company on the little note that Harry had given him at Christmas. Having arranged a time, he set out on the Monday morning. The appointment was for a position in a factory as a time clerk.

After a short tour with the manager, Jamie was offered the job at one pound seventeen and sixpence per week. He was shown round the factory by the factory foreman who showed him where he would be, in his own little office, signing women on and off jobs on the main factory floor. Jamie was happy enough with this and started the next day. As part of his job, Jamie had to ink in the time it had taken for each job to be completed. His maths was good enough and he began to enjoy working.

In the evening, he sat and told Mary just what he had been doing, and she was pleased for him.

They listened, as usual, to the evening news. The news that night was that, at long last, the American forces surrounded at Malmedy and Bastogne had been relieved by their advancing army. The German army had fallen back. The Battle of the Bulge was over.

The V2s were still coming. Originally, these had been launched from Holland. Now they were aimed at Rotterdam not London. They did not want the Allies to have a complete and open harbour where they could bring in supplies for the Allied army. They were now beginning to make inroads in France.

The Allies were having a problem with supplies as their front-line had moved so swiftly forward that the supply line was now several hundred miles long, making it difficult to get supplies to the frontline.

At work, Jamie found that what his father had been doing in his office job was helping complete something called the Mulberry Harbour. This was a floating harbour that was to be towed across the channel, along with several other vessels, which were to be sunk to create a harbour for the D Day landing. Jamie was proud that his father had been involved with the manufacture of such a new idea. The factory where Jamie was working was also making parts of military vehicles. This made Jamie feel that he was involved in the war effort. One thing he didn't miss was standing in a queue in the cold, wet, windy weather with his mother on Saturdays, because now Jamie had to work Saturday mornings.

The family, in general, were now well-settled and looking forward to a time when the war was over.

January moved into February and the weather remained relatively dry. The RAF was now taking full advantage, bombing the German defences, which were now under pressure and heavily bombed, along with all the towns. The casualties were in the thousands.

Mary was finding it a little difficult to keep working while taking Steven to and from school. Steven was far too young to be left to come home or go to school on his own.

The last of the V2 rockets fell on London as the army moved forward and destroyed the launch pads. No more vengeance rockets or V1s fell upon London.

At the end of each week, Jamie went to his mother and gave her his unopened pay packet, from which Mary took her house-keeping money. Mary always left Jamie with seventeen shillings and sixpence. She would take the pound for his keep.

Jamie knew now that he was no longer a boy. He saved ten shillings for six weeks, then on Saturday afternoon, went into Welling to a shop named Fifty Bob Tailors, where he had seen a suit. He swallowed hard and entered the shop. There a man not much older than Jamie. He said, 'Can I help you, sir?' Jamie told him what he was interested in buying. He was measured by the shop keeper to find out if the suit was his size. He just needed his coupons and money. Jamie purchased it. It was the first article of clothing he had ever purchased for himself. He felt very proud that he now owned a suit. It cost him two pounds and ten shillings (50 bob).

When he arrived home, Mary told him to put it on and show her. She said, 'You look handsome, my son. Well done.'

February moved on into March. The very last V2 fell in south-east London but there were no reported casualties.

One evening, after dinner, Mary, Harry and Jamie talked about the future. Mary said that, when the war ended, which, according to the news, wasn't too far off, they could expect the people who owned the house to return from Canada. She had no doubt that they would ask the council for the house to be returned to them. Now she wondered, just what would happen to them? Where could they go? Her mother and father's house would no longer be big enough. Harry said that he thought he should start looking around to see if there was an empty house that he could rent. He thought it would be very difficult, therefore there was little they could do except wait and see what happened.

On the home front, things were beginning to look a lot brighter. More and more food was coming into the country. Still, one had to queue and still, one was on rations.

Some people thought that rationing had made the nation slimmer and fitter. There were no fat or overweight people and everybody appeared healthy, although there were a considerable number of injured. Most of the unhealthy housing estates in central London had been destroyed in the Blitz. Because of this, there were thousands of desperate people looking for somewhere to live.

Over the last couple of months, there had been many battles reported, including the large battle over a bridge at Arnhem. Unfortunately, England had lost many men there and were unable to capture the bridge. The Allied armies had managed to cross the Rhine in several places and forge ahead into Germany. The news was that the Russian forces had also entered Germany from the eastern side and were in Berlin. It was fierce fighting and the German army was crumbling in every direction. The end of the war was in sight.

March moved into April. The fighting was fierce as Germany crumbled under the onslaught of the Russians and the Allied forces. Then came the news that Adolf Hitler and Eva Braun, along with many of the German high command, had committed suicide.

At the end of the first week of April, what was left of the German high command surrendered. The new commanding officer of what was left of their army signed unconditional surrender. World War Two in Europe had ended on the 7th May 1945.

There was still fighting in the Far East against Japan.

On the 8th of August the USA dropped a new weapon on the cities of Hiroshima and Nagasaki. These were the atomic bombs which literally wiped both cities off the face of the earth. Jamie asked Harry, 'What is an atomic bomb that can wipe out a whole city?' Harry explained that he had no idea what an atomic bomb was or how it worked.

On the 15th August, Japan surrendered. The World War had finally ended. Peace in Europe was called VJ Day and the streets of London and all cities were full of people dancing and singing. Large street parties were held.

At long, long last there was no more fear of bombs, V1s, V2s or casualties. That was until the Japanese prisoners of war were found. That was a bad shock for the Allied armies.

The fighting was at last over. Harry said, 'It is gonna take a long, long time for us to get back on our feet. We owe a great debt to the USA and our commonwealth, which will take several decades to clear. It will be years before we get back a semblance of order.'

It became clear that, with such a great number of men being demobbed, Jamie's job was coming under pressure.

Jamie had to leave, but he found work in a tailor's shop.

Mary was also under pressure as men were being given preference for work over women.

CHAPTER 72

IS THIS PEACE?

August came in warm and everyone was looking for a holiday. There was no more worry about warnings or bombs but work still had to go on. This time it was not for the war effort.

The conscription of men for the mines had stopped but miners were still required, as fuel was now needed for both homes and manufacturing goods for the home market.

Germany was divided between the four Allied nations, Russia, France, United States of America and England. Then, because Berlin, the capital, was in the Russian zone, this was to divide into four parts.

It was shortly afterwards that there was tension between Russia and the USA. This was to become known as the Cold War.

Jamie wasn't interested in what was happening in Germany; he was interested in finding out what his future was to be. He told both Mary and Harry that he had decided he wanted to make a career in the RAF but he was underage and had to wait until he turned 16. With their permission, he could join the air cadets in preparation.

Then news about the concentration camps started to be reported. In the paper, there were some graphic pictures.

Jamie stood outside the cinema at every opportunity, trying to get an adult to take him in. This was now common practice by many lads.

One evening, a couple took Jamie in. On the Pathé News, pictures of Bergen-Belsen were shown. Jamie found it difficult to watch the horror that was being shown.

At home, later, Jamie told Harry what he had seen, and said, 'How could men do such things to each other?'

At the end of the month, a general election was held. That was the first time Jamie had seen so many people making speeches and promises about what they were going to do. Jamie wasn't interested in what was called 'politics'. He wouldn't be able to do anything but watch what happened. Eventually the speeches ended and a new government was formed by the Labour Party, as they had won, or so Jamie was informed. Jamie thought, it won't affect me.

On the radio, it was announced that the trial of James Joyce (Lord Haw-Haw), the traitor, was underway. Everyone knew what the verdict would be and that he would eventually hang.

September and October saw the big clear-up of towns and cities.

In November, the radio was full of the big trial that was about to start in a place called Nurenburg in Germany. Many surviving heads of the Nazi party were going to be tried for war crimes. There were so many prisoners, it was thought that it could take a year before anyone knew the outcome. Jamie thought, if they were responsible for what he had seen on the Pathé News, they should all hang.

The rest of 1945 was busy for almost everyone, putting their houses in order or getting the local councils to find housing for the many displaced people, just like Jamie and his family.

The family returned from Canada. Mary, Harry and their sons were told that they had to live in a camp until a house or flat was available.

CHAPTER 73

THE LAST NEW BEGINNING

It seemed to Jamie that it was all about to happen, yet again. The council had given Mary and Harry a new flat in Catford. Both were impressed with it and accepted. Jamie and Steven moved in on 22nd December 1945. Christmas would be a make-do and enjoy as best you can situation.

Harry would have difficulty finding work in the area. Perhaps it would be better after Christmas, Harry said to Mary. Christmas was not an easy time.

Mary said to the rest of the family, as they sat on the floor around the electric fire, 'The council have said they can find us some furniture, from a warehouse in Catford, but as it's holiday time, this may have to wait until the New Year. We have mattresses, blankets and food. There is also the electric oven,' (something Mary had never used and would have to learn). 'I just don't know how we will spend Christmas.'

Early Christmas Eve, Mary and Harry went to a relief centre, taking Jamie and Steven with them. There, they obtained plates, cups and saucers, cutlery, more blankets, pots and pans for cooking. They were all able to have a hot dinner before heading back to the cold, new flat.

With Jamie working with them, they managed to get it all home on that unforgettable Christmas Eve of 1945.

Christmas Day, they had a meagre dinner, sitting on the floor, listening to the radio Jamie had brought with him when they'd left the house. With a cup of tea, Harry's toast was, 'We are alive. Let's hope 1946 is a damned sight better, with God's help.'

CHAPTER 74

1946 – 1948 THE INTERVENING YEARS

This New Year, in 1946, everything seemed so strange, as far as Jamie was concerned. They had this new home, Mary and Harry had to re-establish themselves, somehow, they had to purchase new furnishings, they had to build a new family domain when everything around them was changing. Everywhere there was chaos. There was very little furniture in shops, therefore it was mainly furnishings that had been recovered, spruced up and made to look good. There was utility furniture being manufactured by the government, which was now arriving on the market. Also the council were setting up places to help displaced persons from the bombed and devastated areas. As far as Jamie could see, for England, it was reconstruction of all the damaged towns throughout the land.

There were so many more people about, more vehicles on the road. Life was fundamentally different to anything that Jamie had so far experienced in his short life. The buses were more frequent and there were now trams running through the streets on rails. In some towns, trolley buses were being introduced on electric wires. There were thousands of soldiers being demobbed and there were men looking for work. The place was flooded with men. Buildings were going up everywhere. There were cranes and lorries; all sorts of work in the reconstruction of towns and cities. All this continued throughout the rest of the year.

Before Jamie even realised it, it was coming into December, yet again, with Christmas, followed by the New Year.

January 1947. This was going to be quite a year, as far as Jamie was concerned. Again, he sat and talked with Harry and Mary about what was happening and what his future would be.

Here, again, he said that he wanted to join the RAF. He had lost his job at the tailor's and was now working in a bicycle shop, assembling bicycles. There wasn't a long-term future for him doing this, even though there was now a demand for them. Mary and Harry agreed that they would support his decision, should he still want to take up a career in the services, now that he was old enough to join the RAF cadets.

The weather had become extremely cold. Jamie was working in a shop that didn't have a lot of heating. The weather was causing a great demand for fuel.

In February 1947, there were major power cuts, causing Jamie a great deal of difficulty as he tried to assemble a bicycle in the semi-dark. He just had to get on with the work as he needed the wage for his keep.

At the end of the previous Parliament, just as the war ended, Mr Churchill had said that any member of the commonwealth that had fought in the Allied army was surely entitled to come to this country and settle down, if they so wanted to.

In the June, the first immigrants from the West Indies arrived with their families to settle in England. There was a lot of prejudice shown and a great deal of disturbance because of that. Although Parliament thought this was a good idea, many, many people in England thought otherwise.

In July 1947, it was announced that Princess Elizabeth was engaged to marry Lieutenant Philip Mountbatten, the adopted son of Lord Louis Mountbatten. This was greeted with a great deal of excitement by many people. Jamie took this news in his stride. He thought, I don't know Princess Elizabeth, but could see that a lot of people were talking and rejoicing at this news. All that Jamie knew about Princess Elizabeth was that she was the daughter of King George and that, during the war, she had served in the army. He knew nothing more about her. He made a point of asking both Mary and Harry about the royal family and Mary gave him a full history lesson about the kings and queens of England.

At long last, it was announced that bread rationing had ceased. Now people could buy as many rolls, cakes and other things from the bakery as they wanted, without a ration book.

Everything went on in the same chaotic manner without stop. In Jamie's mind, that had been going on for months now.

In November, it was announced that Princess Elizabeth had married Philip, as planned. There were great celebrations throughout England. A few months later, it was announced that the Princess was expecting a baby, and the child would eventually be the King or Queen of England. Everybody was looking forward to the birth.

The year moved on.

In December, Christmas was celebrated. There were now paper chains and toys available, the Christmas clubs paid out, and both Harry and Mary were able to make a proper Christmas for Jamie, Steven and themselves.

It was at Christmas that Harry remembered his debt to Mary's father. He repaid him, adding an extra five pounds to show his gratitude for the help he had given them all those years before.

In the month of July, the National Health Service came into operation, and a change to national insurance also came into effect. The Labour government nationalised the gas industry. Jamie wondered what nationalisation meant, regarding the National Health Service. What he understood was, it meant that you would be looked after, health-wise, from the day you were born, until the day you died. This was a wonderful idea. Jamie asked Harry if this would help Harry with his leg, and Harry said, 'Of course, yes it will. From here on in, I don't have to worry, because I can always see a doctor, free of charge. Also, I can go to hospital, free of charge, if necessary. The same for your mum, as your mum has something called a goitre in her throat and if the NHS had not happened, she probably would not be getting help or medication to keep her alive.'

Jamie was shocked at this news. He had no idea that Mary was unwell. There was nothing to see. Now, with this news, he was very grateful for this National Health Service.

In the papers of 1948, it was announced that the Olympic Games would be held in August, in London, for the first time since 1936, when it had been held in Berlin. It was to be a great sporting event, played throughout the month. This was the first Olympic

Games Jamie had ever heard about. Mary explained that the last Olympic Games had been held before the war. It was now restarting and would be held every four years. Several English people won gold, silver or bronze medals. Jamie had never heard of the medals that were issued to the winners, whoever they were. He must listen as much as possible to the races on the radio, whenever he could, as it must be interesting, and he wished he could see these games.

It was in the November that the King granted the title Princess of the United Kingdom to Princess Elizabeth. It was on the 14th of the month that Princess Elizabeth gave birth to a healthy son. Again, there was jubilation throughout the United Kingdom. Princess Elizabeth and Prince Philip named the child Charles. The young baby was christened in December.

Jamie had made an application to join the RAF cadets. While attending the cadets, he received his national conscription papers. He was told to attend a recruitment office in London on the 21st September as he had had his 17th birthday. He would be required to have a medical and, should he pass, he would be given a date for enlistment, which would be in 1949.

Jamie attended in September and, as instructed, underwent his medical and was pronounced fit. While he was there, he reported to the Royal Air Force recruitment officer, who discussed with Jamie his reason for wanting to enrol in the RAF. Satisfied that Jamie knew what he wanted, he took note of Jamie's application and his cadet acceptance. He made notes about Jamie details. Then, he told Jamie to get his parents' permission and said that he could sign on as soon as he had them.

Jamie went home and talked to Harry and Mary, who gave their blessing.

It was on 10th January 1949 that Jamie's wish came true and he joined the Royal Air Force. At last, he had warm clothes, hot food in his belly and a very good pair of boots. Who could ask for anything more. This was to last for the next three years at least.

THE END

CPSIA information can be obtained
at www.ICGtesting.com
Printed in the USA
BVHW071227081019
560524BV00001B/59/P